DON'T MAKE ME STOP NOW

DON'T MAKE ME STOP NOW

stories by **MICHAEL PARKER**

ALGONQUIN BOOKS
OF CHAPEL HILL
2007

Published by
ALGONQUIN BOOKS OF CHAPEL HILL
Post Office Box 2225
Chapel Hill, North Carolina 27515-2225

a division of
WORKMAN PUBLISHING
225 Varick Street
New York, New York 10014

Stories in this collection originally appeared in the following publications: "What Happens Next" and "Muddy Water, Turn to Wine" in *Epoch;* "Hidden Meanings, Treatment of Time, Supreme Irony, and Life Experiences in the Song 'Ain't Gonna Bump No More No Big Fat Woman'" and "The Golden Era of Heartbreak" in *The Oxford American;* "Everything Was Paid For" and "Off Island" in *Five Points;* "Go Ugly Early" in *The South Carolina Review;* "I Will Clean Your Attic" in *The Literary Review;* "The Right to Remain" in *The Idaho Review;* "Smoke from Chester Leading Me Down to See Dogman" in *Black Warrior Review;* "Results for Novice Males" in *Backwards City Review.*

"The Golden Era of Heartbreak" also appeared in *The O. Henry Prize Stories 2005.*
"Off Island" also appeared in *Pushcart Prize XXVII* and *New Stories from the South 2003.*
"Hidden Meanings, Treatment of Time, Supreme Irony, and Life Experiences in the Song 'Ain't Gonna Bump No More No Big Fat Woman'" also appeared in *New Stories from the South 2005.*

LIBRARY OF CONGRESS CATALOGING-IN-PUBLICATION DATA
Parker, Michael, 1959 –
   Don't make me stop now : stories / by Michael Parker.— 1st ed.
      p. cm.
   Contents: What happens next — Hidden meanings, treatment of time,
supreme irony, and life experiences in the song Ain't gonna bump no more no big fat
woman — Everything was paid for — Off island — Go ugly early — I will clean your
attic — Muddy water, turn to wine — The right to remain — Smoke from Chester leading
me down to see Dogman — Couple strike it rich on second honeymoon — The golden era
of heartbreak — Results for novice males.
   ISBN-13: 978-1-56512-485-1; ISBN-10: 1-56512-485-5
      I. Title.
PS3566.A683D66 2006
813'.54 — dc22   2006045872

10 9 8 7 6 5 4 3 2

For Jim Clark and Terry Kennedy

ACKNOWLEDGMENTS

I WISH TO THANK the editors of the magazines and anthologies in which these stories first appeared or were reprinted; my students, past and present, at the University of North Carolina at Greensboro; Stuart Dischell, George Singleton, and—in no way least—my editor Kathy Pories, whose help both on and off the page has been endless, careful, gentle, exact, and immeasurable.

Where are my women now, with their sweet wet words and ways, and the miraculous balls of hail popping in a green translucence in the yards?

—Denis Johnson, "Work"

CONTENTS

What Happens Next

I

WHEN HE WAS SEVENTEEN, Charlie Yancey was at a family reunion, skulking around the edges of rooms, his thick hair in his eyes, waves of rather-be-anywhere-but-here insolence rolling off of him like steam, when his father told him to pull the car around, drive his grandmother back to the nursing home.

"Why do I have to?" said Charlie.

"Because if you don't you're not leaving the house for a month."

"Well, fuck me," Charlie whisper-mumbled.

"What did you just say?"

"I said, Well, I need the *keys*," said Charlie.

His father handed over the keys slowly while staring at him slowly and saying slowly as if he was trying not to let himself speed up, "I want you to drop your grandmother off and come straight back here. Do you hear me, Charles?"

"Yes," said Charlie.

"What are you going to do?"

"Force Grandma to withdraw some cash from her bank, stop by the Dot and Dash for a case of beer, swing by and pick up Moocher, and cruise around downtown all night?"

His father looked past him, at something on the wall of the basement, which is where all the teenagers in the family had gathered to play pool. Charlie wondered what his father was looking at but was for some reason afraid to turn his head. He needed his father to hug him or slap him, either one, anything but look beyond him.

"Thirty minutes, Charles," said his father. "That is the maximum amount of time it would take you to get from here to the nursing home and back, even if there was an earthquake. If you are not back in thirty minutes . . ."

His father seemed to grow so visibly and hugely bored with his threat, and his long-running battle with his middle child, who gave him nothing but lip and trouble, that he trailed off and continued staring at the wall, or whatever he was staring at, not Charlie Yancey, not his son, not who he ought to have been looking at.

Charlie shrugged and went to get the car. He had his tapes stashed in the glove compartment. It was his mother's Dodge Dart, a terribly unsexy car to drive if you were a teenager with even a sliver of self-respect. But Charlie had made some improvements. The radio only got AM so he had talked his mother into letting him put in an FM / cassette player with money he made working at Walgreens after school and on weekends. The Dart was parked down the street. Charlie put in Humble Pie's "Smokin'" and cranked it up until the windshield vibrated and the steel doors actually hummed. It cleared his head from all the family melodrama, all the forced pleasantries and smiles. Not that he'd forced it too hard.

"God, Charlie, don't be such an asshole today, okay?" his sister Ellen had said to him that morning when they were waiting around for their mother to finish putting on her makeup. "Just pick one person to be nice to, okay?"

He'd ignored her. Now he sat in the car, nodding to the greasy organ chords of a song called "Hot 'N' Nasty," waiting for his dad to bring his grandmother down to the street. When the song was over he decided he wanted to hear it again on the ride home, so he rewound it and was about to eject the tape when his father appeared by the carport, feeble Grandma Yancey in tow, motioning for Charlie to come up the drive and get her.

"God, do I have to do fucking everything for him?" Charlie said aloud. He got out, fetched his grandmother, ignored his father, who said, "Thirty minutes, Charles." He helped his grandmother in the car, clicked her seat belt around her tiny waist, walked around the driver's side holding his nose at the faint smell of urine he'd detected while leaning in close to her, got in, cranked the car. Twenty seconds of silence followed as he drove to the corner stop sign, put his signal on to turn right, which he was about to do when the opening chords of "Hot 'N' Nasty" came thundering through the speakers. It was much louder than before. He must have accidentally brushed against the volume when he was getting in or out of the car. It was so loud that Charlie thought they'd been hit by another car. Or a train. Maybe the earthquake his father had joked about. It took him a few more stunned seconds to get his act together enough to reach over and turn the volume down. By that time his grandmother was dead.

II

Twenty years later, when he told this story to a woman named Teresa, as they were lying in bed in a motel room alongside an interstate in central Virginia, Yancey held his breath in the silence that followed the word *dead,* which was often oddly reminiscent of that stunned silence that had come over the Dart after he finally managed to turn down Humble Pie. He liked Teresa. Maybe he loved her. Love did not come easy to him—he'd been with a couple dozen women since high school but none for longer than three years and some for as short as a couple months—and he knew from having arrived at this moment before that it was critical, decisive. He needed for her reaction to surprise him. He wanted the questions his story elicited in her to be searingly perceptive and gentle at once. He sort of needed her not to laugh, though, hell, he understood it was funny in a darkly gothic way. She could laugh, it would not blow the door shut on them if she laughed, but if she did happen to laugh it would be best if she did not follow up her laughter with some sort of sitcom dialogue along the lines of, "Omigod, are you serious?"

It would really be better if she did not ask, even reflexively, if he were joking.

Some next questions that it would be best if she avoided:

Did she have a heart attack? In fact, she did, a massive coronary, but it really did not matter much exactly what she died of, given her age and, more important, the fact that the story wasn't really about her death. Still, most people have fairly literal minds. A literal-minded woman was not, to Yancey's mind, very sexy. In fact, if he had to choose between a woman with a little meat on her bones who delighted in abstractions or even drenching irony, and a leggy, taut-stomached beauty who was forever asking him to explain every goddamn quip out of his mouth, hands down the former.

Yet we're conditioned to want the facts. Just a few weeks

earlier, when they'd met in a bar in Richmond, Yancey had asked Teresa where she was from, what she did for a living. (He pointedly did not ask her if she had a boyfriend, as it struck him as immaterial at that point in the game.) These questions were scaffolding. You ask them out of duty and file the answers quickly away. Yancey could not therefore deduct too many points for *Did she have a heart attack?* though if she followed up with more literal questions, say those resembling a medical history taken by a nurse preceding a physical—*Any history of heart disease?*—well, it wasn't as if Yancey were desperate.

What did your dad do to you? Another literal question begged, to be fair, by the way he'd shaped the story, its emphasis on his strained relationship with his father. He didn't mind it so much because it revealed a tendency toward melodrama, which he himself shared, though he was a little ashamed of it and had learned over the years that he was never fully satisfied by the tawdry ending of stories, that the shambles he leaned in close to listen to brought on in him a despair greater than that of the characters themselves. This wasn't always the case. There was a time when Yancey was very nearly soothed by the horrific details of the lives of others. He could not really pinpoint when that period had ended, and sometimes, admittedly, he longed for it to return.

The question also assigned blame. What did he *do to you*? Obviously the asker of this question felt he deserved punishment. In this way it never failed to rankle. Like I fucking killed her, Yancey wanted to say. Though he did in a way. At least some days he thought so. People die all the time because no one pays attention to them, listens to their rather pointless stories. To seventeen-year-old Yancey, his grandmother was ancient, yellow-smelling, her skin like soiled dollar bills he got in change at the backstreet mom-and-pop groceries which sold beer to minors. He did not want to touch her. Even his father seemed vaguely embarrassed by her, not to mention pissed off that he, among his four siblings, shouldered the duty of caring for her. It had taken Yancey many years to realize that his grandmother had a personality—an entire life—preceding the aged state in which he had only known her. Now his father was approaching the same state. The difference was that Yancey had known him before he became creaky and forgetful. Perhaps it was a blessing that he had no children who would grow up to view their grandfather in the dismissive way that Yancey had always thought about his grandmother (when he thought about her at all), but that might well change, depending on the woman lying naked next to him, her response to his story.

He hoped she did not ask *Do you blame yourself for what*

happened? Yancey had no real answer to this question, though he really disliked when people said, in answer to his questions, *I have no idea how to answer that,* for it was Yancey's experience that however fiercely they clung to ambiguity, however slickly they italicized the phrase *Well, yes and no,* they proceeded to deliver glib responses suggesting that they knew very well how to answer that question. One thing Yancey did not want to appear to be was well scripted. In fact, he wasn't all that spontaneous—he thought about conversations he might have with people on the slim chance that he might have them—but by all means he wanted to appear whimsical. Did he blame himself? Look, it was an accident. He forgot to eject the tape, he accidentally brushed the volume control getting out of the car. And at the same time it was all his fault for preferring the oblivion of music over his own family, which admittedly meant more and more to him as he'd grown older himself. Yet he was a teenager. It was in his job description to be self-absorbed, to prefer loud music and locked rooms to some uncle of his discussing his golf game around the dinner table. Shy sensitive teenagers prefer the sanctity of music because it expresses what is for them wholly inexpressible. Sitting in that car, waiting for his father to bring along his grandmother, Humble Pie fucking cranked, Steve Marriott begging some sweet girl to shake that thang, asking Yancey over and over, "Do you get the message?"—twenty years had passed and Yancey still remembered the way that song lifted him above the subdivision where his aunt and uncle lived, treeless and too tight with bland ranch houses. He put his ear to Teresa's shoulder and remembered how those raunchy Wurlitzer chords had sucked him right up on stage in a packed arena, put a mike in his hand, whisked him off stage after the encore into a waiting chartered plane. How could he be blamed for craving such sweet deliverance?

Though he could not say it did not hurt him to think about that day, or hurt to retell the story. It didn't hurt him where his listeners assumed: his heart. The heart, to Yancey, was a swimming-pool pump. It served roughly the same function as a hot-water heater. Since that day his grandmother's had given out, Yancey had come to detest the mawkish association of the heart with emotion. What others called heart, Yancey located outside the body. It was in the air, molecular, shifting like dust motes. Perhaps it was in this motel room, that rarefied and elusive substance falsely consigned to the chest. Yancey guessed he'd very soon see.

Can you listen to Humble Pie now? This was usually phrased as a statement—*I bet you've never been able to listen to that song since*—but it was a question all right. He could not really discount it, as it was, at root, serious, more serious perhaps than those who posed it realized. The indestructible tendrils of the past, come snaking back to encircle if not strangle us—that was what this question was about. How do you get over anything? Are distraction and forgetting the only path to peace? One girlfriend of Yancey's freaked when he revealed, absentmindedly, that the leather jacket he favored in winter had been a gift of his ex. The fact that he wore the jacket was proof that he was not "over" this ex, according to his girlfriend. But it's just a jacket, said Yancey. It's warm, plus it's just now getting broken in good. How could he ever bear to hear Humble Pie again, much less the history-laden "Hot 'N' Nasty?" The argument that it was only a song—that it had a terrific rhythm section, that Steve Marriott's vocals were whisky-soaked brilliance, that if you flat-out failed to shake your ass to it you had no ass to shake—was not worth offering to that stupendous portion of the population, male and female, who believed the heart was something more than a pumping station. You just could not tell these people that, in fact, you liked to listen to "Hot 'N' Nasty" a couple times a month and expect them to see you as anything less than a monster.

Oh Teresa, please surprise me. I want you to be different, therefore you will be different. For one thing, she waited a long time after he told the story before speaking. This was a good sign. The story demanded lag time. The longer she waited, though, the more hopeful Yancey became, the more pressure he applied to her question. Which is why it hurt so deeply—hurt in a place very near where he took his breath—when she asked the one question no one had bothered to ask him before, the one he did not ever want to answer.

"What," said Teresa, her voice a little croaky from disuse (which only made Yancey want her more), "happened next?"

III

The turn signal clicked. Yancey's grandmother slumped over, her mouth open a little. He knew instantly that she was dead, but how? He'd never seen death before, except of course on movie screens. She could have been sleeping but for the un-natural loll of her neck. He felt, instead of panic (which he figured was on its way), a sense of warmth, of peacefulness, for both of them. He looked to the left and to the right. The road was clear. He looked in the rearview mirror; there was no one behind him. To the left and to the right: clear. He put his foot on the gas.

Yancey had had twenty years to think about what happened next, and he'd turned it over in his mind so many times that he had assigned an image to the turning: sugar spinning on a stick, gathering into a cloud of cotton candy. Like cotton candy, the versions of those moments following the unexpected and lethal blast of "Hot 'N' Nasty" had been deceptively inviting, disappearing rather tastelessly with each compulsive nibble. Sugar and air, empty calories. Yancey did not care for cotton candy, nor for images of his mind obsessing over what finally was a series of lefts and rights, tap of the brake and slap of the gas pedal. Once he had read an article about a famous French theater critic that spoke of "the ulcer of consciouness: the mind devouring itself." The phrase needled him when the stick was thrust into the cotton candy chamber, as did the fact that the French theater critic ended his days in an insane asylum, no doubt eating his own excrement, as famously insane Frenchmen are prone to do.

To narrate, for sweet Teresa, what happened next without baggage, to tell it exactly as it happened, free from the self-conscious renderings bathed in the unnatural pinks and blues of artificially colored cotton candy, free from footnotes about insane Frenchmen, free from revision, hyperbole, lies: if he could just pull it off, he'd never have to tell this story again.

He drove a mile or so before his grandmother, jolted as he slowed for a curve, fell forward in such a way that made her look, well, dead. Her chin grazed her breastbone, her arm flopped over toward his side. Yancey pulled off onto Carolina

Avenue, which he knew to disintegrate into a two-track leading to a dumping ground by a ravine. In the woods he stopped at the turnaround, leaned his grandmother over so that her head rested against the window glass. Strangely he did not mind touching her. The heat from the hot-water heater that is the heart had not yet leaked out of her. Her joints were still pliable. She was dead and it was his fault, but he felt calm and oddly focused. A purpose was unfolding, though he did not yet know what it was. However, it was noble and rather simple.

Dusk had been slowly gathering, and with it a chill that Yancey felt because he'd cracked his window to combat an odor growing hard to ignore. He remembered just minutes ago holding his nose at the faint smell of urine. What a wuss I used to be, said Yancey to his grandmother. He took side roads, welcoming the anonymity of darkness, for riding around was the principal form of teenaged entertainment in his town, and people knew his car.

Yancey pulled behind the Dot and Dash, alongside the Dumpster, where no one could park next to him. His grandmother's purse lay on the seat between them. He only took a five.

Old Cedrick was behind the counter. He'd sell booze to a third-grader. Yancey grabbed three tall Bulls from the cooler.

Cedrick said, "You think you're a soul brother?"

Yancey said, "You know you're a bigot?"

Cedrick wrinkled his nose. "Boy, you stink," he said. "What's that smell?"

Yancey stood at the counter, his change in his hand, trying to think of a comeback. But then he remembered that he was not alone.

"Hey man, you take care."

"Say what?" said Cedrick. He seemed disappointed, but Yancey had remembered his sister begging him to pick just one person to be nice to.

"Have a good night. Nice talking to you. Hey, I love your store."

"Boy, get the fuck out of here now before I call the law on your smelly ass."

In the car the odor was worse. Yancey rolled down the window. He zipped up his windbreaker. He put the change back in his grandmother's purse. He did not *need* the beer to do what he was about to do, but it would not hurt. At least it was what his father expected of him. He did not want to disappoint his father.

Yancey drank the first beer before he even reached the city limits. He tossed the can in the floorboard at his grand-mother's feet. He burped, then excused himself. Out toward

Beamon's Wood, the tight series of S-curves beckoned. He finished his second beer and threw the can out of the window near Pope's Pond, accidentally. He thought about going back to get it, but it was dark and he was talking to his grandmother. Some days it seemed he was still talking to her, still in the car, high on Schlitz Malt Liquor, driving around the back roads, had been for twenty years. Often he was confused about what he'd told her recently and what he'd said back then, which wasn't really a problem as this was the nature of time—collapsible, flexible, unreliable. He told her how wonderful it would be to get everyone together—all the people he'd failed, the ones he'd loved and who had loved him however briefly—and have a big party in the woods. I would like to feel, just as long as the party lasts, the attraction that drew me to them in the first place, and them to me. You know, before things fell away. Before whatever it is out there in the air, that thing you people call *heart,* turned back into dive-bombing mosquitoes and swamp fog and dust kicked up from the tractor trailers on the highway. Grandma, how do you make anything last? He chugged his third tall boy as they approached the tightest switchback out by Beamon's Wood. He'd been obeying the speed limit and actually slowed down as they entered the curve. It wasn't as if he wanted to die, too—though to be honest he did not really give much thought to what injuries he might sustain. Whatever happened was fate—even though he engineered it. The contradiction did not bother him because it was his fate, according to his father, to screw things up. But how could it be his grandmother's fate to be killed by a fat blast of organ, bass, and drum? She deserved better. The road curved to the left, but Yancey and his grandmother, engrossed in conversation, drove intently into the pine forest.

IV

There was something deeply sexy to Yancey about telling someone you maybe love and whom you want to love you back your darkest secrets. Like sex following funerals and excruciating hangovers, the love you make after such a revelation is punctuation, an impassioned if desperate attempt to prove you are, in fact, very much alive. Therefore Yancey, in the silence that followed his answer to her question, moved in close to Teresa, trilled his fingers sweetly in the gaps between her ribs, as if striking a complicated chord on an instrument of which he was an acknowledged master, and listened with his entire body for an answer.

She still hadn't said anything. He had always found it odd that the others had merely accepted the end of the story as offered. Oh, they had their questions, the ones Yancey had hoped Teresa would not ask, but they'd finished the story for themselves, jerking Yancey out of the car, having him run back to his aunt's house, frantic and shaken, where they had him tell his father exactly what happened and nobly suffer the consequences. And he had never bothered to correct their version, which meant that he could not stay with them.

Teresa, well, she did not pull away from his touch. But nor did her body encourage his. It occurred to him that she might think his interest in her at this moment creepy, inappropriate, but he was willing to take that risk, for the moment he described had taken place twenty years earlier, and if it had ruined his life it was only because he had let it. If, in this silence, Teresa were pulling slightly away from him—so slightly she did not even realize it, as if his story, like rain atop a mountain, had begun an erosion that would ultimately wear them down to nothingness—well, what could he do about it?

Yancey thought of what he did not tell her. It was something she wouldn't believe, something so freaky he often wondered if he'd made it up. As they'd come to rest against a pine tree, the car, miraculously, was still running. Some part of one of them—his grandmother's arm, Yancey's knee—had nudged the tape, which he'd ejected at the stop sign, back into the player. Yancey's head had hit the windshield hard, leaving a spiderweb of splinter cracks; his forehead was warm and wet with blood. His grandmother had come unlodged from the position he'd taken such pains to place her in earlier, and was also bleeding, her neck twisted crazily so that she was inclined toward him, looking at him expectantly. How could he ever share with anyone that moment when "Hot 'N' Nasty" took right up where it had left off, in midlyric, as if every day had its own irrepressible sound track, and this song, however inappropriate, belonged to Yancey and his grandmother on the day of her unscheduled departure. They sat there listening. Yancey's legs throbbed. Later he would find that he'd cracked a femur and broken a leg and bruised three ribs, but the pain, at that point, was not located so much in the body as outside the car, in the woods, in the world. There it mostly remained, so many years later, despite Yancey's attempts to bring it back inside, to inhale it and let it out like the synchronized breath of lovers.

"Hidden Meanings, Treatment of Time, Supreme Irony, and Life Experiences in the Song 'Ain't Gonna Bump No More No Big Fat Woman'"

IN THE SONG "Ain't Gonna Bump No More No Big Fat Woman" by Joe Tex, the speaker or the narrator of this song, a man previously injured before the song's opening chords by a large, aggressive-type woman in a disco-type bar, refuses to bump with the "big fat woman" of the title. In doing so he is merely exercising his right to an injury-free existence thus insuring him the ability to work and provide for him and his family if he has one, I don't know it doesn't ever say. In this paper I will prove there is a hidden meaning that everybody doesn't get in this popular Song, Saying, or Incident from Public Life. I will attempt to make it clear that we as people when we hear this song we automatically think "novelty" or we link it up together with other songs we perceive in our mind's eye to be just kind of one-hit wonders or comical lacking a serious point. It could put one in the mind of, to mention some songs from this same era, "Convoy" or "Disco Duck." What I will lay out for my audience is that taking this song in such a way as to focus only on it's comical side, which it is really funny nevertheless that is a serious error which ultimately will result in damage to the artist in this case Joe Tex also to the listener, that is you or whoever.

"About three nights ago/I was at a disco." (Tex, line 1.) Thus begins the song "Ain't Gonna Bump No More No Big Fat Woman" by the artist Joe Tex. The speaker has had some time in particular three full days to think about what has occurred to him in the incident in the disco-type establishment. One thing and this is my first big point is that time makes you wiser. Whenever Jeremy and I first broke up I was so ignorant of the situation that had led to us breaking up but then a whole lot of days past and little by little I got a handle on it. The Speaker in "Ain't Gonna Bump No More No Big Fat Woman" has had some time now to go over in his mind's eye the events that occurred roughly three days prior to the song being sung. Would you not agree that he sees his life more clear? A lot of the Tellers in the stories you have made us read this semester they wait a while *then* tell their story thus knowing it by heart and being able to tell it better though with an "I" narrator you are always talking about some kind of "discrepancy" or "pocket of awareness" where the "I" acts like they know themselves but what the reader is supposed to get is they really don't. Well see I don't think you can basically say that about the narrator of "Ain't Gonna Bump No More . . ." because when our story begins he comes across as very clear-headed and in possession of the "facts" of this "case" so to speak on account of time having passed thus allowing him wisdom. So the first thing I'd like to point out is Treatment of Time.

There is a hidden meaning that everybody doesn't get in this particular Song, Saying or Incident from Public Life. What everybody thinks whenever they hear this song is that this dude is being real ugly toward this woman because she is sort of a big woman. You are always talking about how the author or in this case the writer of the song is a construction of the culture. Say if he's of the white race or the male gender when he's writing he's putting in all these attitudes about say minority people or women without even knowing it, in particular ideals of femininity. Did I fully understand you to say that all white men author's basically want to sleep with the female characters they create? Well that just might be one area where you and me actually agree because it has been my experience based upon my previous relationships especially my last one with Jeremy that men are mostly just wanting to sleep with any woman that will let them. In the song "Ain't Gonna Bump No More No Big Fat Woman," let's say if you were to bring it in and play it in class and we were to then discuss it I am willing to bet that the first question you would ask, based on my perfect attendance is, What Attitudes Toward Women are Implied or Explicitly Expressed by the Speaker or Narrator of this Song? I can see it right now up on the board. That Lindsay girl who sits up under you practically, the one who talks more than you almost would jump right in with, "He doesn't like this woman because she is not the slender submissive ideal woman" on and on. One thing and I'll say this again come Evaluation time is you ought to get better at cutting people like Lindsay off. Why we have to listen to her go off on every man in every story we read or rap song you bring in (which, okay, we know you're "down" with Lauryn Hill or whoever but it seems like sometimes I could just sit out in the parking lot and listen to 102 JAMZ and not have to climb three flights of stairs and get the same thing) is beyond me seeing as how I work two jobs to pay for this course and I didn't see her name up under the instructor line in the course offerings plus why should I listen to her on the subject of men when it's clear she hates every last one of them? All I'm saying is she acts like she's taking up for the oppressed people when she goes around oppressing right and left and you just stand up there letting her go on. I'm about sick of her mouth. Somebody left the toilet running, I say to the girl who sits behind me whenever Lindsay gets cranked up on the subject of how awful men are.

Okay at this point you're wondering why I'm taking up for the speaker or narrator of "Ain't Gonna Bump No More" instead of the big fat woman seeing as how I'm 5'1" and weigh 149. That is if you even know who I am which I have my doubts based on the look on your face when you call the roll and the fact that you get me, Melanie Sudduth and Amanda Wheeler mixed up probably because we're A: always here, which you don't really seem to respect all that much, I mean it seems like you like somebody better if they show up late or half the time like that boy Sean, B: real quiet and C: kind of on the heavy side. To me that is what you call a supreme irony the fact that you and that Lindsay girl spend half the class talking about Ideals of Beauty and all how shallow men are but then you tend to favor all the dudes and chicks in the class which could be considered "hot" or as they used to say in the seventies which is my favorite decade which is why I chose to analyze a song from that era, "so fine." So, supreme irony is employed.

As to why I'm going to go ahead and go on record taking

up for the Speaker and not the Big Fat Woman. Well to me
see he was just minding his own business and this woman
would not leave him be. You can tell in the lines about how
she was rarin' to go (Tex, line 4) that he has got some respect
for her and he admires her skill on the dance floor. It's just
that she throws her weight around, literally! To me it is her
that is in the wrong. The fact that she is overweight or as the
speaker says "Fat" don't have anything to do with it. She keeps
at him and he tells her to go on and leave him alone, he's not
getting down, "You done hurt my hip once." (Tex, lines 25–
27.) She would not leave him alone. What she ought to of
done whenever he said no was just go off with somebody else.
I learned this the hard way after the Passage of Time following Jeremy and my's breakup. See I sort of chased after him
calling him all the time and he was seeing somebody else and
my calling him up and letting him come over to my apartment and cooking him supper and sometimes even letting
him stay the night. Well if I only knew then what I know
now. Which is this was the worse thing I could of done. Big
Fat Woman would not leave the Speaker in the song which
might or might not be the Artist Joe Tex alone. Also who
is to blame for her getting so big? Did somebody put a gun
to her head and force her to eat milkshakes from CookOut?
Jeremy whenever he left made a comment about the fact that

I had definitely fell prey to the Freshman Fifteen or whatever. In high school whenever we started dating I was on the girl's softball team I weighed 110 pounds. We as people nowadays don't seem to want to take responsibility for our actions if you ask me which I guess you did by assigning this paper on the topic of Analyze a Hidden Meaning in a Song, Saying, or Incident from Public Life which that particular topic seems kind of broad to me. I didn't have any trouble deciding what to write on though because I am crazy about the song "Ain't Gonna Bump No More" and it is true as my paper has set out to prove that people take it the wrong way and don't get its real meaning also it employs Treatment of Time and Supreme Irony.

One thing I would like to say about the assignment though is okay, you say you want to hear what we think and for us to put ourselves in our papers but then on my last paper you wrote all over it and said in your Ending Comments that my paper lacked clarity and focus and was sprawling and not cohesive or well organized. Well okay I had just worked a shift at the Coach House Restaurant and then right after that a shift at the Evergreen Nursing Home which this is my second job and I was up all night writing that paper on the "Tell-Tale Heart" which who's fault is that I can hear you saying right now. Your right. I ought to of gotten to it earlier but all that aside what I want to ask you is okay have you ever considered that clarity and focus is just like your way of seeing the world? Like to you A leads to B leads to C but I might like want to put F before B because I've had some Life Experiences different than yours one being having to work two jobs and go to school full time which maybe you yourself had to do but something tells me I doubt it. So all I'm saying is maybe you ought to reconsider when you start going off on clarity and logic and stuff that there are let's call them issues behind the way I write which on the one hand when we're analyzing say "Lady with the Tiny Dog" you are all over discussing the issues which led to the story being written in the way it is and on the other if it's me doing the writing you don't want to even acknowledge that stuff is influencing my Narrative Rhythm too. I mean I don't see the difference really. So that is my point about Life Experiences and Narrative Rhythm, etc.

The speaker in the song "Ain't Gonna Bump No More No Big Fat Woman" says no to the Big Fat Woman in part because the one time he did get up and bump with her she did a dip and nearly broke his hip. (Tex, line 5.) Dancing with this particular woman on account of her size and her aggressive behavior would clearly be considered Risky or even Hazardous to the speaker or narrator's health. Should he have gone ahead and done what you and Lindsay wanted him to do and got up there and danced with her because she was beautiful on the inside and he was wanting to thwart the trajectory of typical male response or whatever he could have ended up missing work, not being able to provide for his family if he has one it never really says, falling behind on his car payment, etc. All I'm saying is what is more important for him to act right and get up and dance with the Big Fat Woman even though she has prior to that moment almost broke his hip? Or should he ought to stay seated and be able to get up the next morning and go to work? I say the ladder one of these choices is the best one partially because my daddy has worked at Rencoe Mills for twenty-two years and has not missed a single day which to me that is saying something. I myself have not missed class one time and I can tell even though you put all that in the syllabus about showing up you basically think I'm sort of sad I bet. For doing what's right! You'd rather Sean come in all late and sweaty and plop down in front of you and roll his shirt up so you can gawk at his barbed wire tattoo which his daddy probably paid for and say back the same things you say only translated into his particular language which I don't hardly know what he's even talking about using those big words it's clear he don't even know what they mean. I mean, between him and Lindsay, my God. I loved it whenever he said, "It's like the ulcerous filament of her soul is being masticated from the inside out," talking about that crazy lady in the "Yellow Wallpaper" (which if you ask me her problem was she needed a shift emptying bedpans at the nursing home same as that selfish bitch what's her name, that little boy's mother in the "Rocking Horse Winner.") You'd rather Sean or Lindsay disrespect all your so-called rules and hand their mess in late so long as everything they say is something you already sort of said. What you want is for everybody to A: Look hot and B: agree with you. A good thing for you to think about is, let's say you were in a disco-type establishment and approached by a big fat man. Let's say this dude was getting down. Okay, you get up and dance with him once and he nearly breaks your hip, he bumps you on the floor. Would you get up there and dance with him again? My daddy would get home from work and sit in this one chair with this reading lamp switched on and shining in his lap even though I never saw him read a word but "The Trader" which was all advertisements for used boats and trucks and camper tops and tools. He went to work at six, got off at three, ate supper at five thirty. The rest of the night he sat in that chair drinking coffee with that lamplight in his lap. He would slap me and my sister Connie whenever he thought we were lying about something. If we didn't say anything how could we be lying so we stopped talking. He hardly ever said a word to me my whole life except, "Y'all mind your mama." Whenever I first met Jeremy in high school he'd call me up at night, we used to talk for hours on the phone. I never knew really how to talk to anyone like that. Everything that happened to me, it was interesting to Jeremy or at least he acted like it was. He would say, "What's up, girl?" and I would say, "nothing" or sometimes "nothing much" and I would hate myself for saying nothing and being nothing. But then he'd say, "Well what did you have for supper?" and I'd burst into tears because some boy asked me what did I have for supper. I would cry and cry. Then there'd be that awful thing you know when you're crying and the boy's like what is it what did I say and you don't know how to tell him he didn't do nothing wrong you just love his heart to bits and pieces just for calling you up on the telephone. Or you don't want to NOT let him know that nobody ever asked you such a silly thing as what did you eat for supper and neither can you come out and just straight tell him, I never got asked that before. Sometimes my life is like this song comes on the radio and I've forgot the words but then the chorus comes along and I only know the first like two words of every line. I'll come in midway, say around about "No More No Big Fat Woman." I only know half of what I know I guess. I went out in the sun and got burned bad and then the skin peeled off and can you blame me for not wanting to go outside anymore? She ought to go find her a big fat man. The only time my daddy'd get out of his chair nights was when a storm blew up out of the woods which he liked to watch from the screen porch. The rain smelled rusty like the screen. He'd let us come out there if we'd be quiet and let him enjoy his storm blowing up but if we said anything he'd yell at us. I could hate Jeremy for saying I'm just not attracted to you anymore but hating him's not going to bring me any of what you call clarity. Even when the stuff I was telling him was so boring, like, then I went by the QuikMart and got seven dollars worth of premium and a Diet Cheerwine he'd make like it was important. Sometimes though he wouldn't say anything and I'd be going on and on like you or Lindsay and I'd get nervous and say, "Hello?" and he'd say, "I'm here I'm just listening." My daddy would let us stay right through the thunder and even some lightning striking the trees in the woods behind the house. We couldn't speak or he'd make us go inside. I know, I know, maybe Jeremy got quiet because he was watching "South Park" or something. Still I never had anyone before or since say to me, I'm here I'm just listening.

I'm going to get another C minus over a D plus. You're going to write in your Ending Comments that this paper sprawls lacks cohesion is not well organized. Well that's alright because we both know that what you call clarity means a whole lot less than whether or not I think the speaker in the song "Ain't Gonna Bump No More No Big Fat Woman" ought to get up and dance with the woman who "done hurt my hip, she done knocked me down." (Tex, line 39.) I say, No he shouldn't. You say, Yes he should. In this Popular Song, Saying, or Incident from Public Life there is a Hidden Meaning that everybody doesn't get. Well, I get it and all I'm saying is you don't and even though I've spent however many pages explaining it to you you're never going to get it. If you get to feel sorry for me because I come to class every time and write down all the stupid stuff that Sean says and also for being a little on the heavy side I guess I get to feel sorry for you for acting like you truly understand a song like "Ain't Gonna Bump No More No Big Fat Woman" by the artist Joe Tex.

In my conclusion the speaker or the narrator of the song "Ain't Gonna Bump No More No Big Fat Woman," a man previously injured before the song's opening chords by a large aggressive type woman in a disco type bar refuses to bump with the fat woman of the title. In doing so he is merely exercising his right to an injury free existence. Treatment of Time, Supreme Irony and Life Experiences are delved into in my paper. There is a hidden meaning in this Song Saying or Incident from Public Life. Looking only at the comical side is a error which will result in damage to the artist and also to the listener which is you or whoever.

Everything Was Paid For

THE FIRST TIME it was cashew nuts. Not something that Clay could say he'd ever craved, but he thought it best to start with something small. He could work up to the watches, which he could sell to Peterson or trade for crank. Bulova, Seiko, Timex, Swatch, Japanese digital, which wouldn't bring jack on the street but maybe if he gave them to Peterson, Peterson would trust him enough to front him again. It had been a while since Peterson fronted him, even longer since anyone had trusted him.

Neal Marshburn moved behind the soda fountain. Clay watched him wait on the customers. Wait he seemed to take literally, his laziness echoed in the slap of his shoes against the rubber floor runner. The longer the line the more he dawdled, stopping once to talk on the phone while Clay waited behind a bony boy resting his nose on the counter, quarters he'd saved for a Cherry Coke readied in his free fist.

Marshburn's blond hair was cropped in a bristly crew cut, and his outfit was standard-issue prep: starched khakis, blue oxford, shoes designed for sailors beloved by landlubbing college boys. He looked no different since he'd gone off to college, not that Clay had paid him much attention before. He was just another kid in his high school, back of a head in a clogged corridor, pimply neck and cocky walk, jean-jacketed arm draped stiffly around some fuzzy-sweatered blonde. Maybe they'd talked at a party. Maybe they'd happened to lurch together down the steps of some middle-of-a-muddy-field trailer, bragging about the sizes of their buzz-ons before stumbling off in different directions to water furrows. Maybe. Clay couldn't say he remembered Marshburn all that well. He was only nineteen and already there'd been a lot of people passing by that it didn't hurt anything to forget.

Judging from the sparseness of merchandise on the shelves, Clay wondered if this drugstore was on the verge of going out of business. He'd never been in there before. He'd noticed the place—it was right across from the hospital where Linda's mother worked as a nurse. He'd spent some bored time in the lobby over there, waiting for Linda while she visited her mother. She was there right now in fact, up in the OR lounge trying to talk money out of her mama before another case came up: some poor stomach wound, hysterectomy, appen-

dix. That's the way they referred to folks up there according
to Linda's mama, not by names but by what was wrong with
them. Linda said they'd be riding through town and all of a
sudden her mama would go, There's that hernia we did last
week, and point to a bald-headed banker putting money in a
meter. Linda loved to talk about her mother's job; Clay hated
hearing it. He wasn't squeamish when things were in his face,
but secondhand skinny about people he didn't know, that
weren't names or numbers but amputations and C-sections
and golf-ball-size kidney stones—why did Linda think it was
so interesting?

Clay spotted Ruth Crosby making her way to the front
of the store and for the first time, too late, Clay thought of
what to do if Marshburn didn't wait on him. Clay had gone
out with Ruth years ago when they were both too young to
know what to do but did it anyway without looking or saying
much. He sometimes hung out with her husband who moved
pot for Peterson, too.

"Just looking," Clay told Ruth when she said hello and
asked him if he needed help. She just looked away from him,
out the plate glass at the afternoon beyond the store, beyond
the salaried hours ticking away too slowly. Clay felt bad for
her, for everyone with a boring job, for everyone with a job.
Except Marshburn, a rich college kid who didn't need to work

in the first place. Remembering Marshburn, Clay felt the hate that made his marrow turn to mist. Slack hate he called it, the worst of his various flavors and shades.

Ruth was making small talk, something about her husband off on a fishing trip. Be nice to her, something in Clay said. Not neccessarily a voice of his; something from somebody else's life maybe, somebody in this store passing close enough to cross wires with, like those faint voices that sometimes lace phone calls.

"Let him know when you decide," Ruth said, and when she walked toward the back of the store Clay made his move on Marshburn, who was leaning against the counter, drinking a Coke. When Clay tapped a dime on the counter, Marshburn smiled stiffly and nodded.

"How ya doing, man?" He seemed embarrassed. He knows, thought Clay, but how could he? Or maybe he's ashamed to be seen working behind the soda fountain.

"Half a pound of cashews," said Clay. Marshburn went off to scoop and weigh. Clay was glad to be alone, as next to Marshburn he felt grungy, dressed in a black T-shirt and army fatigues he'd pinched from a clothesline one night, which he'd wrenched tight with a belt so they wouldn't hang off his ass. He was sweaty from the bus ride and his hair hung lank and oily to his shoulders; he'd wrecked the apartment earlier, searching for something to put his hair back with, but

Linda had claimed to be out of elastic bands again and the butcher had already snagged his newspaper from the lawn so Clay couldn't swipe the rubber band like he usually did. Maybe they sold hair supplies here, Clay thought as Marshburn appeared with a bag already oil-dappled, folding the top down and ringing up the sale.

Marshburn set the bag down. Clay laid a dime beside it and stared at the clock above Marshburn's head. Marshburn grinned at the dime, as if he thought Clay could not count.

"Dollar twenty-five," he said.

"You know Linda Grimes?"

"Linda Grimes? Yeah, maybe," said Marshburn. "She go to Central with us?"

"She didn't finish," said Clay.

"Knew her in ninth grade, I guess it was," said Marshburn.

"She told me."

"I think I had, like, English with her or something," said Marshburn.

"Mrs. Saul. Fourth period. You borrowed a book from her once."

"You were in there, too?" Marshburn grinned again: What a horrible memory I have, his grin suggested. College knowledge had replaced all this sophomoric trivia about high school—who was who, what classes they shared.

"*We Have Always Lived in the Castle,*" said Clay.

"Say what?"

Clay repeated the strange title slowly. "That's the name of the book you borrowed."

"I guess," said Marshburn, shrugging, looking past him for other customers, but there were none.

"One twenty-five," he said.

"She sat in front of you."

"I kind of remember her but not real well."

"But the desks were real close."

"Why are you telling me all this?"

"And your hands were real long."

"What'd she tell you?"

Clay tapped his dime against the counter.

"How am I supposed to remember what you're talking about?" said Marshburn.

"Same way she did?"

"I don't know what you're trying to say, plus I'm busy . . ."

Clay leaned in close, breathing big to calm himself. "I don't get summers off. You get fucking summers off forever."

"What do you mean?" Marshburn affected a laugh and turned his palms out, pantomiming innocence. "I'm working. I work here, I get paid for this. This is a business, right? You have to pay for stuff in this store."

"Thank you," said Clay.

"I don't even know what you're talking about," said Marshburn. A group of junior high kids wandered up from the back
booths and Marshburn and Clay broke off their conversation
so abruptly that someone watching might have thought they
were kin.

WALKING INTO THE hospital lobby Clay let his
features go forlorn long, as if he'd just lost a relative or was
preparing to sit vigil for such loss. He picked this up from
everyone around him, morose-looking country people with
wax-paper skin. They wore their Sunday clothes, and their
heavy brown shoes spotted the vacuumed-combed carpet like
muddy rocks in a freshly disked field. Going gray-faced and
sullen was Clay's usual mode while waiting here for Linda,
and it did not come totally from the people around him; these
trips to the hospital to beg money off of her mother always
made him feel impotent and ashamed.

He searched the nooks of the lobby, hoping to see Linda
slumped across a couch in one of the tucked-away little living rooms, a *McCall's* or *Southern Living* splayed across her
chest. No doubt she was still upstairs stocking up on oper-
ating-room horror stories. Another reason he never went up
with her was because Linda's mother always went off on him
about jobs: Get a job, where's your job at, you still too good to

work? After a couple of visits he waited downstairs, napping on one of the couches in the lobby.

They always took longer than he liked, these visits with Linda's mom, and were never to Clay's thinking cost-effective. Linda'd come down with fifteen bucks grocery money or, worse, a check written out to the landlord, which neither of them could figure out how to convert into ready.

But last time—about a month ago—something had happened that made up for all the times they'd come away with pocket change. They were waiting for the bus at the stop in front of the hospital, slumped away from each other in determined silence. Only twenty bucks to pay the power people and her mom insisted on sealing the check up with the bill Linda'd had to produce to get the cash. All of a sudden Linda had seen Marshburn walk across the street and into the drugstore, and before she even realized what she was doing—she would admit as much later—she'd told Clay about Marshburn.

"See that guy?"

There had been a lot of guys around. Clay was sulking about the power bill, which he'd hoped would be in the form of green instead of one of Mrs. Grimes's hokey checks, pink-topped mountains rising behind her loopy cursive. He could understand why she chose them, of course—they made her money look casual, an adornment, while those plain blue or green checks revealed the desperation of her finances.

"That guy" would of course turn out to be another there-goes-Joe's-gallbladder. Yeah, Clay said, not bothering to look up.

"Neal Marshburn," she'd said, and without a noticeable change of tone, she told him the whole story.

How she told her story affected Clay more than the facts. Her tone was flat, but the nitty-gritty seemed to Clay real seventh grade as to terminology. "He felt me up down below," she said. Clay looked up from passing traffic at Linda, then to the double-glass doors where Marshburn had disappeared. This particular phrase made him pay attention.

"Up down below?" He couldn't resist a little sarcasm in repeating it, though he wanted to be gentle now. Instead he was livid: his slack hate loosened, rendering him invertebrate, a mass of molten anger on the bus bench. Linda stood when their bus rose slow motion over the crest of the hill, but he threw his arm out like a crossing guard.

"We'll take the next one," he said. "Tell me more now."

She'd sat and sighed and told him how it started, the book with the weird title Marshburn had borrowed from her in class, more details—information about the room, the subject studied, her blue hip-huggers with red faded stars.

"Tell me exactly what he did to you," Clay had said. Linda looked up the street in the direction that their bus had disappeared then down the street in the direction of the next one. She appeared tiny beside him, her feet on the bench, arms hugging her shins, chin resting heavily on her knees. He saw how sorry she was that she'd said anything. We missed the bus, the switch and dart of her eyes told him; now we're stuck here for another half hour. He'd been with her long enough to tell when she thought he had given in to his hate.

Or maybe she was over it, had managed to put it out of her mind. After all, six years had passed. That she had pushed it away would be seen by some as a triumph. But how had she been able to do this, and why? Then and there on the bench Clay decided that it had to be unfinished, that it was unfinished.

"Really, Clay. This was ninth grade."

"You're saying he didn't know better?"

She stared across the street instead of answering. She'd slumped on the bench, her legs far enough apart so that guys passing in cars might be able to get a shot of her underwear. Clay started to tell her to sit up, but he was distracted by the plate glass window of the drugstore touched by the afternoon sun, its glints and twinklings an indecipherable semaphore Clay felt on the verge of interpreting.

"You can get arrested in ninth grade," he said. "And do time. Juvenile, but it's still time."

"I never wanted to get him arrested, I just wanted him to stop sticking his hands down my pants during English class."

He could tell he was losing her, that if he didn't slow down she'd shut down, probably forever.

"You ever told anybody else?"

"Didn't do any good," she said.

They sat in silence until the bus arrived. Sitting in the back on the way home, Clay had seen not bus seats but carved desks, aisles of them packed tight in a steamy-windowed classroom. Scaly radiator ticking beneath a windowsill, chalk dust smell; sitting an aisle over from Linda and Marshburn, he'd watched the whole thing in slow motion, while up in front behind the wobbly lectern Mrs. Saul talked transitive verbs.

NEXT TIME IT WAS CANDY: assorteds in a box heart-shaped and wrapped in pink lacy paper, gone bad according to the expiration date. Clay searched a half hour for something he wanted. All the merchandise was dusty, the stuff near the front windows sun-dyed, items near the back moldy as if they'd been brought up from a bomb shelter. Marshburn had seen him come in and was ignoring him, herding a thick hill of dirt down the warped floorboards with a push broom.

Air-pillow insoles? Shaving cream? Clay could find nothing he wanted, and getting things he needed—hair bands for instance—seemed sleazy. As he stood by the candy rack, weighing packages in his hand, cellophane crackling, Marshburn started up the aisle. Good, thought Clay when he discovered the expired box, I can return this later and get my dime back.

When he felt Marshburn approaching he stepped into the aisle, blocking the way. Though the broom and the advancing flank of dirt stopped at Clay's shoes, the cloud of dust preceding it continued, billowing up the aisle.

"Can I get some help here?" asked Clay.

Marshburn nodded to the pharmacy counter, where Ruth Crosby worked a register.

"She's open," he said, curling the line of dust into a clump and herding it around Clay's feet and up the aisle. Clay waited until Ruth was free, small-talked a minute about her job, husband, parties they'd heard about, Linda.

"Can you call Mr. Marshburn over here?" he said finally.

"Mister Marshburn? You mean Neal? What do you need him for?"

"I need to ask his advice on something. Man to man."

Ruth laughed so loud that Clay was stunned. Rippling out over the aisles, her laugh caused nearby customers to swivel their heads and smile toward Clay and Ruth.

She looked down at the box of candy Clay held below the

counter. "You need some supplies, right? That's the word guys use when I wait on them that kills me the deadest."

"I ride bareback, Ruth. You should know that."

Ruth kept her smile but froze it, stretched out the corners of her mouth until it was the generic eight-to-five smile of a salesclerk. In the space of ten seconds she seemed ten years older. "It's hard to remember these things, Clay. Like, do you remember every meal you ever ate in your life?"

"Just the ones that stood out," said Clay. Ruth laughed again, as loud as before, but this time her laughter drew no smiles from passersby.

"Obviously you're not embarrassed to buy rubbers from a girl like me."

"It's not about rubbers, Ruth. Really, girl, get your mind out of the gutter."

Ruth gave him another insincere smile. "That's the gutter to you, I guess. So what do you want with him? Advice on an athletic support?"

"You ask a lot more questions than I remember."

"I'm a lot more curious about things than I was when I was hanging around you."

"You act like his lawyer. Just call him over here."

Ruth looked over at Marshburn. "Well, he's not doing anything but leaning on his broom."

Watching Ruth talk to Marshburn, the two of them sneaking glances at him from across the store, Clay wondered if there was something between them he could use.

"I just couldn't bring myself to let anyone else wait on me," Clay said to Marshburn when he shuffled over to the counter.

"Not even an old friend?"

"Me and you are old friends. We went to the same high school. That makes us fellow alums."

"I didn't even know your name until Ruth told me," said Marshburn, staring at the candy.

Clay put the candy down on the counter and said his name aloud, extending his hand to Marshburn. Marshburn loosened his grip when he felt the moist dime in Clay's palm.

"Pleased to meet you," said Clay.

Marshburn pulled his hand away without the dime. "Prices have gone up since last week."

Clay nodded at the candy. "This is a present for Linda Grimes. From you."

"Not that again." Marshburn sighed and looked away. "I'm telling you nothing happened."

"So I shouldn't believe her?"

"I'm just saying I don't remember anything like what she said happening. She sat in front of me, yeah. I remember talking to her sometimes. But that's been five or six years."

"Statute of limitations run out?"

"I didn't do anything."

"I'm inclined to believe her, since I live with her and all."

"Well," said Marshburn. He looked around the store for help, but people—customers and employees both—moved obliviously through the tight aisles with their heads down. Watching them, Clay understood that this could go on forever. No one here cared.

"Can you gift wrap this?" he asked Marshburn.

"I can't just keep giving you stuff. They'll find out and fire my ass."

"Okay, fine. Just put it in a bag. You don't even need a card. I'll tell Linda it's from you."

Marshburn pushed the dime back across the counter. "Don't come in here again," he said.

Clay took the bag Marshburn handed him but left the dime on the counter. "Oh, no, I want to pay for it. I wouldn't feel right if I didn't pay for it."

BACK AT THE APARTMENT Linda ate the candy quickly, as if she suspected it was stolen and was trying to destroy the evidence.

"Tastes kinda old," she said when she was halfway through the first layer.

"I'll take it back," said Clay.

Linda lifted the brown plastic tray from the box and peeked beneath, studying the next layer. "Where'd you get it anyway?"

They were sitting at the small table in the kitchen. Life indoors was for them a series of moves from kitchen table to bed, rectangle to rectangle. They hated the low-ceilinged apartment they rented, a converted garage that sat in the back of a retired butcher's yard. Every day they got up and got out of there, unless the weather was bad—they didn't have a car—or Clay was working for Peterson and they had customers coming by. Most of the time they had someplace to go—the unemployment people for Linda's check, Clay's probation officer, the hospital—but when they had a free day, they'd ride the number 14 bus that took the ferry across the sound to Bell's Island, where they'd eat oranges and lie on the beach fully clothed, or break into a boathouse and sit there for hours watching the water wave, as if the sound was a privately screened movie, the boathouse their own box seat.

When Clay told her where he'd bought the candy, Linda reached for the half-empty top tray but did not try to fit it back into the box.

"You didn't see that guy Marshburn I told you about."

"As a matter of fact," said Clay.

Linda pushed the candy away and said Clay's name. There

was a stack of bills on the table that Linda brushed with the box and toppled, and watching them fan out across the Formica Clay thought of how he always made Linda pay bills or, more often, made her write out the notes requesting clemency. They would sit at the table, Linda licking stamps and the crescent gluestrips of envelopes between her sentences, as if even the words they exchanged were broken up, interrupted by what they lacked. They were being made to grovel; their life was carved into little rectangles, rooms and past-due notes. No longer could it be cashews and assorted chocolates.

"Marshburn sold me the candy," said Clay, though he knew he didn't need to.

"You didn't say anything to him about what I told you." When she got anxious, Linda abandoned the interrogative, as if turning questions into statements could quell doubts.

Clay looked down at the candy, thinking of how to turn this thing around so that she could see that he was looking out for her.

"Goddamn it, Clay. That happened a hundred years before you."

"About the time this candy was made."

"Right. Make fun. Okay. Let somebody stick their hands down your pants every day for three months."

At times like this it was as if there was a script already

written for him, words in reserve that he didn't even think about as he spoke them. When things got heated, desperate sentences came not from him but from places he'd been before where such things were said—cars speeding down back roads, the back rows of classrooms, the parking lots of bars.

"Sounds good," he said. "Bring it on."

Linda left the table, slamming the thin door to the bedroom. Now the script again, rising as involuntarily as blushing skin. "Why didn't you tell anybody? Tell the teacher? Your mom? They could've stopped it." When no answer came he knew he should stop, but he felt off balance, down one. Her silence was a trump.

"He claimed you wanted it," yelled Clay, and at once he both regretted saying it and felt as if it delivered him power, even if summoned from someplace false but instinctive, someplace anyone could tap into, someplace shared.

"No candy today," said Clay. "No nuts."

Marshburn tipped a cup of soda and crunched his ice. "Nothing for you at all unless you got some cash."

"I need a box of syringes," said Clay.

Marshburn smiled. He shook his head like a teacher mock-tired of an unruly pupil's antics. "See the pharmacist when he comes back from lunch. Of course you gotta have a prescription for those things. And I'm not authorized to sell them to you even if you had one."

"You know where they are, though."

"Sure," said Marshburn. "But that doesn't mean I can just walk back there and grab a box."

"I'll wait here."

Marshburn, filling his cup with soda, stared at him as if he were deranged. But then something passed over his face and he grinned, as if they were together on entirely different ground. "Be right back," he said, and he disappeared.

While Marshburn was gone, Ruth appeared to work his register. She looked at Clay with pity, and when he tried to small-talk her, she stood there with a frozen can-I-help-you cast to her face.

"I'm being helped," Clay said, and stood aside. He lurked by the back booths until Marshburn returned.

"Here you are, sir," Marshburn said, handing Clay a bag. "If they're not the right size you can return them." Halfway to the front door, Clay cringed when Ruth called out, "I thought there was only one size."

PETERSON WAS SO PLEASED with the syringes that a day later he fronted Clay three pounds of weed. "We're in the money again," Clay said to Linda after Peterson left. "No more sponging off mama, no more having to listen to her creepyass stories. No more flipping the coin."

They flipped a coin to decide whose family to hit up first, even though heads or tails it was always a trip to the hospital, since Clay's parents had all but disowned him after his second bust and his brothers and sisters practiced something called tough love. As far as Clay could figure, this tough love meant that they could claim to be helping him help himself by clamping tight their wallets and pocketbooks, not answering their doorbells when he came around for a visit.

"We don't even have a coin to flip. We'd have to draw broom straws," said Linda.

Clay patted the cellophane bags of pot. "With some of this dough I'll get us a roll of quarters."

"That's what I call planning for the future," said Linda.

"Peterson trusts me now."

"Because you got him some needles he trusts you." He didn't try to hide it from her; it was hard to hide anything in their two tiny rectangles, visible or invisible, physical or emotional. She'd been sitting at the kitchen table reading a magazine when Clay had come in with the bag, the logo of the pharmacy clear to her. "Did you steal those or are you blackmailing him?" she had asked.

"He wants to make it up to you," said Clay. Saying this

didn't make it true, but it did make it easier to believe. "So he's going to be helping us out right along through now. During these leanest of times."

Linda had put her magazine down. "Remember when I suggested spending the night with Larry in exchange for back rent over at the other place? And you freaked out?"

"To start with you were eighteen then, not fourteen. And that was something you were willing to do, not something somebody was forcing you to do."

"Willing is not really the word I'd use. But anyway, Clay, if it's so different in your eyes, how come you didn't let me do it?"

"Because I'm not a pimp and you're not a whore. This isn't about money, Linda. You were fourteen years old when he did those things to you. I think you must have blocked it out of your mind."

"I remember everything about it," said Linda. "And I think about it a lot. Like how I passed him notes telling him over and over to stop. I even lent him my English notes, which he paid June Miller to copy out for him I found out later. And after a while I'd turn around in the middle of the class and tell him to quit it and everybody heard, everybody in the whole class knew, I told the teacher who didn't do a goddamn thing and told Mom who talked to the teacher who talked to him again and he still didn't stop it."

"It sucked back then," said Clay. "Nobody listened to a thing you said."

"At least everything was paid for," she said.

Clay looked confused.

"No flipping coins to find out where to go beg. No rent, no bills, no bitchy secretaries at the unemployment office treating me like I'm lying and lazy and ignorant."

"That's fucking crazy, Linda."

Linda's look was like a poke at some obscure animal of the sea that had washed up on shore. A prod to see if it was still alive. "Forget about him, Clay. This isn't yours, okay?"

"He said you wanted it, remember? I got to make him pay for that." Another lie, but one made right by his promise to avenge it.

"What if Marshburn had gotten a summer job lifeguarding instead of at that pharmacy?" Linda said when Clay came back from Peterson's and pushed enough cash across the table to take care of that month's bills.

"We'd have some serious suntans," said Clay. "It doesn't matter where he works, Linda. There's something bigger than this day-to-day. What he owes you and all. But you have to hit him in the day-to-day if you're going to hurt him. Otherwise you can ask all you want for justice and respect and what you'll get is I'm sorry, I won't do it again, I didn't realize what I was doing. This way we make sure he really pays."

Clay watched Linda reach for the cash. He thought she was going to count it, start to divide it up and place it into envelopes, but she clutched the bills and looked down at the table.

"You hear about those college guys who get drunk and go off on those sorority girls?" said Clay. "The newspapers give it a special name, what these college boys do: date rape, they call it. Personally that makes me a little mad. Like you have to be a certain kind of girl to get date-raped."

Linda looked up from the pile of money in her hand.

"That didn't come out right," said Clay. "What I mean is have you ever heard of a date rape in this part of town? You ever heard of anybody getting date-raped west of Eagle Street?"

Linda spoke very slowly. "First of all, no one west of Eagle goes out on dates. Anyway, you're trying to get me to quit talking about Marshburn. What I want to know is, are you keeping up with how much he owes? Do you decide or does he? When does this stop, Clay? When he gets caught taking those needles?"

"I'd say that'd be a natural end."

"And you get popped for receiving stolen goods."

"Those packages barely touch my hands. In my possession an hour at most. Let 'em prove it."

This day marked the beginning of much strange behavior from Linda. One minute she'd rue the moment she told Clay about Marshburn, the next she'd get all defensive and say that she'd done nothing wrong by admitting it, that it was Clay who had taken her troubled past and turned it into trouble looming in the future for both of them. But he'd silence her always with shopworn words he felt uncomfortable with but that worked, not necessarily by comforting her but by sending her out of the room in disgust. And there was money coming in to distract them now.

Like always, the money seemed as if it was going to last forever, and Clay did nothing to earn it but pick up an occasional package and hang around the house to receive customers. No more trips to the hospital, no more trips to the pharmacy either. He'd long since worked out an arrangement with Marshburn: Clay would call and let him know when he wanted more syringes, and they'd arrange a place for Marshburn to drop them.

One afternoon Marshburn suggested bringing them over to the apartment. The fact that he almost agreed shocked Clay into remembering what this thing was all about. Marshburn's complicity, which Clay had put off confronting for fear it would end, began to bother him again. Who decides how much he owes? Linda had wanted to know. Lately Peterson favored him over all the other guys he called his subcontractors, and Clay felt sure that he would continue to trust him even after the syringes stopped coming. Ditching Marshburn would certainly make Linda happy, though a part of Clay still resented her whining about a situation he'd managed to turn around. She owned three string bikinis now, just for laying out in the butcher's yard on a beach towel; she couldn't even swim. Still, now seemed as good a time as any to break it off with Marshburn. Clay arranged to meet him later that night at a bar out on South Boulevard.

Clay was sitting at the end of the bar, sipping a draft, when suddenly, Marshburn was there beside him. "What're you drinking?" he asked Clay.

"Alcohol," said Clay. But he had to fight an urge to be decent, which surprised him; one of the more consistent things in his life was his ability to hold a grudge. "Where's the package?" he asked.

"In the car," said Marshburn. He tapped Clay's almost empty mug. "Another one?"

"Sure," said Clay. Why not? Marshburn was paying. While Marshburn stood beside him trying to get the bartender's attention, Clay allowed himself to wonder how Marshburn was getting away with this. Surely someone kept up with syringes sold, especially if it took a prescription to get them. Maybe Marshburn was tampering with the records somehow, or paying for them out of his own pocket. Maybe he really did feel guilty for what he'd done to Linda. Why else would he be doing this? If Marshburn was motivated by guilt, Clay could still consider himself the enforcer, making Marshburn pay for his sins. What was really wrong with making a little cash in the process? When bosses put the move on their secretaries and got dragged into court over it, the system awarded these women big bucks. For emotional and psychological distress. You can't buy back innocence; might as well get a condo out of it or, in Clay's case, a couple of months rent on an ex-garage and Peterson's trust.

This idea pleased him so much that he was swept away for a quarter hour while Marshburn bought him beers. Once Clay caught a reflection of the two of them in the mirror behind the bar and noticed what a strange pair they made: tanned Marshburn with his polo shirt and khaki shorts, Clay in his black jeans and tank top, his body pale and a little puddly from weeks of sitting around the apartment rolling samples for clients and watching endless hours of tube.

Marshburn was talking about the drugstore when Clay came back into the conversation, how the owner underpaid everyone there and treated them like dirt, how Ruth threatened every day to quit. Marshburn said he was glad this was only a summer job; he couldn't think of spending the rest of his life, even the rest of the year, slaving away in a place like that.

The way he claimed to feel sorry for Ruth, yet in the next breath was glad to be getting out, aroused Clay's hatred. He had come here to tell Marshburn to fuck off and here he was drinking with the guy, listening to him whine. He studied Marshburn's hands, which held a sweaty beer but had once disappeared down Linda's pants.

"Why are you doing this?" Clay said. "Why are you going along with me? Because of what you did to Linda?"

Marshburn slid his mug around on the bar, leaving watery trails. His cocky smile seemed intended to offer Clay a variety of reasons.

"Why the hell else would you?" said Clay.

"Hard not to steal from a place that pays what that asshole does. It's harder to steal syringes of course, there's paperwork involved, but hell, he sells them all the time and forges the papers, so why shouldn't I?"

"You stole from there before?"

Marshburn laughed aloud. "Everybody does. I bet Ruth hasn't bought any shampoo in a year and a half. Toilet paper, razor blades, whatever."

While Clay considered his great act of retribution, Marshburn lowered his voice and began talking, eyeing a table of girls across the room but aiming his words into Clay's ear. The words leaked from his mouth like smoke and hung about them in clouds, and even though Clay had come here with his own script written and ready to deliver, the thought of Ruth's bathroom cabinet crammed with stolen toiletries took his words away. Marshburn ordered another round and tapped his bottle against Clay's; the clink of glass seemed absurdly loud to Clay, rising above bar chatter, jukebox and the crack of pool balls, and when it finally died down Clay asked Marshburn to run it all down for him again and craned to hear the words which would tell him what to do, how to make this pay.

Marshburn's car was a junker: seats sprung and coils exposed, tufts of colored batting filling the air every time Clay shifted in the seat. Clay sneered as Marshburn cranked the radio up with a few twists of a socket wrench. The boy was obviously slumming. Clay knew of other rich kids who drove beat-to-shit cars to be funky, for a joke.

"What's your dad do, Marshburn?"

"Repairs typewriters," Marshburn said rotely, as if he'd been asked this a thousand times and all the reluctance to tell had seeped out with the first nine hundred. Clay started to ask about the mother, but he realized that it didn't much matter. If the dad repaired typewriters, the mom was not likely to be running for mayor.

Marshburn had not gone a block before he whipped into a convenience store, hopped out, and left four words lingering in the car with Clay—"beers for the road." This was the way Clay and Peterson used to do it—hit a bar for a few hours, then cruise the streets with a six until all their fear was watered down.

Marshburn had left the car running, and its ragged idle drew stares from others waiting in cars parked close. Clay watched Marshburn palm a six from the cooler and slink drunkenly up to the counter. He thought of something Linda said a few weeks ago, how in the middle of class she used to turn around and hiss at Marshburn to stop. He wondered if some people in that class, in their school, and all across the city referred to Linda in the way that her mom described her patients, as That Girl Neal Marshburn Used to Feel Up in Ninth Grade.

As they cruised, Clay downed two beers and looked out the window, grunting occasionally in response to the things Marshburn said. Marshburn wasn't horrible, though he talked too much. He'd started up about Ruth, not so veiled references to the extended lunch hours the two of them took.

Clay kept quiet, which seemed to make Marshburn more brazen.

"You used to go out with her, too, I hear."

"That was years ago," said Clay.

"Hard to remember that far back, right?"

Clay felt like bolting from the car, though they were doing fifty at least. He fell silent, wondering how he could back out, but the thought of the look on Marshburn's face when Clay made his lame excuses kept him quiet.

Marshburn parked a few stores down from the drugstore. They got out of the car at the same time and moved off in the shadows to take leaks against opposite sides of a Dumpster. Marshburn talked the whole time, but his words were unintelligible, even when the sounds of their streams dwindled from a steady metallic pelt to a dull drumming and, finally as their bladders emptied, a dribbling in the dirt. Clay was too jittery to listen; he hadn't done this since he'd been caught doing it, sent to jail for it. Hell, he was still on probation because of it. It was something he said he'd never do again, but that was before Marshburn.

He thought of sending Marshburn in alone, but earlier in the bar it became clear that Marshburn didn't know the good stuff when he started talking 3 mg phenobarb. Aspirin, stuff they give to neurotic cats. And Diazepam—pink and heart-shaped, valentine candy. If someone was going in, might as well go for the controlled. When Marshburn said he'd never noticed any cabinet, Clay wrote him off as hopeless. Once inside, he'd make him use his hands. Marshburn was wasted enough to leave his prints around like clothes cast off after a late-night binge.

They stood in the shadows for a long time, Clay half-listening to Marshburn describe in too great detail this air-conditioning duct idea of his. He sputtered describing it, as if it was some great secret. This is like a game to him, Clay realized, like Linda sitting in front of him in her blue hip-huggers in fourth-period English.

"You're sure we can get through?"

"I was just in there. Asshole owner made me check it out to make sure something wasn't blocking it. He thought the re-pairman screwed it up instead of fixing it. Thinks everybody's lying to him, trying to get over on him."

"Let's do it then," said Clay. He pushed away an image of Linda at home asleep, her head at the foot of the foldout the way they had to lie to keep the skeleton of the frame from pressing into their own bones. Maybe he would clear enough dough here to get them out of that box or at least buy Linda that water bed she'd wanted. He sought out the script to tell him what he was doing was right, and alongside Marshburn the words came easily. Underneath the store they crawled through the cool dirt, pipes grazing their heads and chunks of rock and concrete digging into their palms. Marshburn sparked a plastic lighter to find the duct. In darkness again, Clay heard the aluminum of the duct pop under Marshburn's weight. Filling his lungs with fresh air, he climbed in after him.

They crawled through the dark. Once Clay whispered to Marshburn, How much farther, and he immediately felt whiny, like a kid strapped into the backseat of a station wagon. The darkness inside the duct was so total that moving through it did not seem like moving at all; something else was moving, something inside of Clay, something deep and barely fathomable, which he'd never felt before. When the whoosh came, Clay thought at first that it came from inside his head, beer buzz and nervousness and the changes of the last few weeks combining and combusting, producing this noise that would blow in lines to trade with Marshburn from the script they shared. It was only after the chilled blast hit that Clay realized that the air-conditioning had clicked on.

Marshburn was startled, too. He stopped crawling and hunkered, and when Clay ran into him he began to flail, sweeping his arms back and forth as if he was being attacked.

When Marshburn's hand brushed his forehead, Clay recoiled in the darkness. There he cowered, longing for a way to suspend himself in the frigid breeze so as not to touch the metal walls, which gave to his touch like yielding flesh but were cold enough to burn.

Off Island

AFTER SO MANY STORMS hit the island the people started
to move away. In the end it was only Henry Thornton on one
side of the creek, Miss Maggie and Miss Whaley on the other.
Sisters: Miss Maggie with her dirty same old skirt and Henry's
old waders she used to slosh across the creek, Maggie hugging
on him nights when she got into her rum and came swishing
down to his place to hide out from her sister. Henry hid out
from Miss Whaley himself, stuck close to his house down the
creek where his family had stayed since anyone could remember. Three bodies left on the island and a Colored Town right
on until the end. Every day Henry would cross the creek up
to where his white women lived: sisters, but Miss Maggie had
got married and could go by her first name instead of Whaley
which her older sister by three years clung to like the three of
them clung firm to their six square miles of sea oat and hum-
mock afloat off the elbow of North Carolina.

Across the sound it got to be 1979. Henry's oldest boy Crawl gave up fishing menhaden out of Morehead to run a club. He wrote Henry that he'd purchased this disco ball. Miss Maggie read the letter out to Henry on the steps of the church one warm night. Henry told her, Write Crawl, tell him send one over, we'll run it off the generator in the church, hang it up above the old organ, have this disco dance. Henry made a list in his head of everybody he'd invite back, all of them who'd left out of there after Bertha blew through and took the power and the light. Crawl wrote how that ball spinning under special bulbs would glitter diamonds all up and down your partner. Miss Maggie snickered, said, I ain't about to take a letter and tell him that. Imagine what Whaley would do come some Saturday night when we're dancing in a light bound to suffer her a hot flash. Up under his breath Henry said, We? Ain't no we. In his head he was twirling his Sarah around in a waterspout of diamonds. Tell everybody come back for the disco, Crawl, he wrote in his head. All of his eleven children and Miss Maggie's son Curt, the prison guard, up in Raleigh. Hell, Crawl, invite back those Coast Guard boys and some of the summer people even. He was sealing up his letter when he looked out across the marsh to where night came rolling blue black and final over the sound. He ripped that letter open and crossed it all out and said instead, No thank you, son, to some disco ball, we got stars.

Every morning Henry poled his skiff out into the shallows to fish for dinner. He stayed out in good weather to meet the O'Neal boys bringing in the mail off the Cedar Island ferry. Be sure you give me all them flyers, he'd say every time, and the O'Neals would hand him a sack of grocery store circulars sent over from the mainland advertising everything. Miss Whaley liked to call out the prices at night. "They got turkey breast twenty-nine cent a pound." All it took to make Henry wonder how come he stayed was to sit around long enough to hear Whaley say this three times a night about a two-week-old manager's special one hundred miles up in Norfolk. Crawl was always after him to move off island, had come after him six times since Bertha. You don't got to stay here looking after the sisters daddy till they die or you one. Come on, get in the boat. Crawl showed up wearing his hair springy long and those wide-legged pants made out of some rough something, looked like cardboard, to where your legs couldn't breathe. Boots don't ought to come with a zipper. Why would Henry want to climb in any boat with duded-up Crawl? He would keep quiet watch his grandbabies poking around the beach and going in and out of the houses standing empty waiting on their owners to come back, sitting right up on brickbat haunches pouting like a dog will do you when you go off for a while. He would watch his grandsons jerk crabs out the sound on a chicken liver he give them and having themselves some big easy time until they hit that eye-cutting age. Look at Granddaddy fussing after his white women, what for? Henry would look at them not looking at him and hear the words out of Crawl's mouth all across the Pamlico Sound and all the way back. Your granddaddy don't want to change none. That island gonna blow and him with it one of these days.

What would Henry Thornton be across the sound? Now, who? This he could not say but it wasn't what they all thought: scared to find out. Maybe fear was what kept the sisters from leaving, though they had their other reasons. Maggie would do right much what her big sister said do when it came down to it. Miss Whaley stayed on partly for the state boys who came down from Raleigh every spring before the mosquitoes rode the land breeze over. Every April a boatload of them, always this fat bearded one with his bird glasses and often a young white girl who asked most of the questions. They'd get the answers up on a tape machine, so Henry called them the Tape Recorders. Miss Whaley'd put on her high-tider talk the Tape Recorders loved to call an Old English brogue. They said Henry spoke it too, though how he could have come out talking like an Old English, they didn't tell him that. He didn't ask. He didn't care to talk for them, but it didn't matter much because Miss Whaley loved a tape recorder. Every year she'd tell them about her father's daddy got arrested in Elizabeth City because he favored the man shot Abraham Lincoln who was loose at the time. She didn't mention he was over there on a drunk. Sometimes Maggie would, though, and cackle right crazy loud. Miss Whaley every time would tell about Henry's younger brother Al Louie Thornton who cooked for the guests over at the first lodge before it washed away and who was known over the island for wearing bras and panties and shaved his chest hairs and plucked around his nipples and painted his toenails. Sometimes he'd cook in his apron and shirt and that's all. Babe Ruth came over to hunt, they took him back in the kitchen to meet Al Louie. Babe Ruth took Al Louie's autograph, though Miss Whaley left that part out, too.

One year the tiny white girl pulled Henry aside, said, That lady's digging dirt all the way around your family tree, Mister Henry, serves her right if you want to return the favor. Wanting Henry to tell it on a tape machine, Miss Whaley almost getting married three times and then falling all over Miss Maggie's, her own sister's, husband, the no-fishingest man ever born on island and some said a thief. Henry could have taped that and more. He could have had Miss Whaley showing her white ass in some book right alongside Al Louie's black-aproned ass. But he just gave that little girl a smile and said, I don't no more hear her than the wind after seventy-some years on this island and last six with just us three.

The Tape Recorders were all the time trying to get Henry to act like he hadn't ever been off island much at all. He played them like they wanted, even though he'd spent two years at the Coast Guard base up in Weeksville and six years in the Norfolk shipyards. There he took up welding and did decent at it. Now his children reached right up the East Coast to Troy, New York, like stops on a train. Morehead, Elizabeth City, Norfolk, Baltimore, Philly, Newark, Brooklyn, up all the way to Kingston and Troy. He'd took that train many times when Sarah was alive. She loved it off island. All the time talking about moving, retiring she called it. But what was there to retire from? Wasn't any after to sit down from on this island. Henry came back to the island a damn good welder but what was it to weld? Can't weld conch shell, seaweed, fishbone. He bought some pigs and chickens off his brother and later on two milk cows from the O'Neals and got by selling crabs and flounder to O'Neal who turned right around, sold to the wholesalers in Hatteras for what Henry knew was some serious profit.

Two storms before Bertha, the one that opened up a new inlet down on the southern tip of the island, Sarah bled to death on the kitchen floor. Henry had got caught over in

Ocracoke on errands for the sisters and what it was was the wind. Henry'd tacked the kitchen on himself out of washed up timber mostly and some he'd traded the O'Neals for, which wasn't much better grade than what the tide brung up. And Henry's hand-hammered kitchen falling, slashing a hole in his Sarah's forehead. Sarah lying on the floor in the rain, her blood running the brown boards black. Before he left he'd asked the sisters, y'all check up on Sarah while I'm gone. Sarah wasn't nearly as friendly with them as Henry. Maybe because they were women and it had got down to four of them, three women and one man to run man things. Sarah did not stomach Miss Whaley's attitude and as for Miss Maggie's mess when she took a drink and came right up close enough to Henry to blink cross-eyed (maybe because at that particular nearness he won't even black just blurry), well, Sarah knew it. She studied everything but didn't say one word to Henry about it even though he knew when she knew something, he could read her just like he could the wind and the sound and the sky. If Henry wasn't there to drag her across the creek nights she'd have stayed home singing those gospel songs Crawl's wife taped her off the radio. They had the lights then and Sarah favored this Al Green she said had a voice smooth as liver. Maybe she was singing her Al Green right up until Henry's kitchen came down on her and do you

know the timber he cobbled that kitchen out of blew right
off island? Ocean brung it to him, wind took it away. And
left Sarah lying out on the floor holding a pair of scissors in
her hand, what for? What was she fixing to cut? The sight of
those scissors drove Henry crazy. He pried them out of her
fist and flung them into the inlet and tried not to look at her
head whichways upside the stove.

She wouldn't let me go after her, Miss Maggie told Henry
talking about Whaley, which Whaley herself was big enough
to admit. Why lose two to save one? she said. Sarah bled to
death and it turned up big-skied sunny like it will do after a
storm to make you feel worse and the sun dried the blood on
the floorboards until it looked like paint. Toting the wood
down island is how he discovered the new inlet. And in his
mind it was Sarah cut the island in two. Sheared right through
the marshland with her sewing scissors. Low tide he'd walk
over to the good-for-nothing-but-birdshit southside. He'd
crouch and smoke him an El Reeso Sweet if he could get one
off the O'Neals. Wasn't one thing over there worth seeing but
he knew Sarah was wanting him where the sisters weren't.

But he couldn't be hiding all day down island. They would
be wanting their mail. Henry would pole out and the O'Neals
would tie him up if they won't in a hurry and pass him a Miller's High Life. They liked to get him talking about the sisters.

He knew they went right back to tell it all over Ocracoke and said how he was getting something off Miss Maggie and Miss Whaley liked to watch, he'd heard that, it got back to him. Brung back on the wind maybe. From his house down by the inlet you could see across to Ocracoke the winking lights of Silver Lake and the lighthouse tossing its milky beam around but neither Henry nor the sisters crossed over unless one got bad sick. The O'Neals brought groceries and supplies which Henry mostly paid for with his catch, Whaley being too tight to part with what money left the sisters from their daddy who even the Tape Recorders knew to have gotten filthy off a load of Irish whisky washed ashore on Sheep Island in the twenties. Whaley when she paid him at all was so ill mouthed about it Henry stopped asking. Sarah used to collect on it and because she knew Sarah was not scared of her, Whaley always paid her what she owed. Henry wasn't scared of neither of them but it seemed like with only three of them on the island and him keeping the two of them alive he could leave off acting the nigger and one way to do that was not go knocking on Whaley's door asking for anything he didn't leave over there the night before. Sometimes Maggie would pay him in dribbly change and yellow-smelling dollars she stole and hid God knows where on her person, but it wasn't enough to make much of a difference.

Across the water Crawl wrote claiming it was 1980. He says you're seventy-five this year, Henry, Maggie said to him one night on the steps of the church. Miss Whaley sitting in her lawn chair had her flyers to go through, she wasn't listening. When she had her newspapers spread out across her lap on the church steps where the three of them would sit just like people in town will linger after supper to watch traffic and call out to neighbor women strolling babies, she was just not there. Would a two-storied green bus come chugging across the creek, she wouldn't have lifted her head to grace the sight with her reading glasses. Henry thought at first she was loosening her grip, preparing to go off island by teaching herself what to expect to pay for a pound of butter across the water in 1980. But after four or five years he figured the flyers were part of what kept her here. She'd spit the prices out like fruit seed. She'd get ill at a bunch of innocent bananas for costing highway robbery, she would read her prices like Maggie would read the letters to the editor, taking sides and arguing with every one of them, My Land the way people live in this world, she'd say every night when it got too dark to read, and she folded up her newspaper like the Coast Guard taught Henry to fold a flag, that careful, that slow, like a color guard was standing at attention waiting on her to finish.

Crawl don't know nothing about how old I am, Henry said to the water.

Old enough to know better, said Maggie. She tugged at his shoelace while her sister studied the paper above them. Henry always sat on the second to bottom step and Miss Maggie'd start out on the top step and slide down even with him as the evening settled, though her sister would rustle prices to try to halt her.

Too old to change, what it is, said Miss Whaley.

Henry swatted the back of his neck loud, but he didn't come away with any bloody mosquito because it was a sea breeze and there wasn't any bite. His head was getting ready to switch around and stare out Miss Whaley over her paper and he backslapped himself to keep still. The slap rang out like a hammering. Miss Whaley cleared her old throat. Miss Maggie to cover up got on with Crawl's letter, but Henry didn't listen anymore. In his head he started his own letter to the sisters, one he knew he'd never ever send them even if he could write. Y'all ought not to have done me like y'all done me, he wrote in the first line, and that was as far as he got.

That night he lay talking to Sarah in the dark. He told her what Miss Whaley said and he discussed it. How come she talking about me not changing when it's her sitting up in her throne reading out her numbers on and on. Why you let that white woman hurt you so, Henry, he heard Sarah say. He heard her words like he heard the surf frothing on the banks, making its claim and then receding, taking it back, offering more words. A conversation. Sarah used to say to him, You the strongest man I ever met, you can work all day and all night if you care to and not make a noise about it to nobody. I seen you sit outside shucking corn in a nor'easter and you ain't scared of anybody who'd pull a knife on you. How come you let what people say get away with you so much? And Henry never answered, though he knew how bad people could hurt him with what they said. He just hurt. He'd been knowing that. Maybe that was why he stayed on this island so long after everybody left and there wasn't anyone to hurt him anymore but Miss Maggie who was too sweetly dizzy in the head to hurt much and Miss Whaley who he thought he knew every which way she had of hurting him but she was good for coming up with a new one. Henry just hurt. Sometimes it didn't take anybody saying anything to him to his face, he'd remember what one of the men he used to fish with said to him sixty years before when they were boys swimming naked in the inlet and he'd be out in his skiff all by himself and he'd want to put his head down in his lap and let all the crabs and oysters and mackerel and blues and tuna go on about their business. He didn't care about reeling in a thing. Hurt nearly bad enough to let everybody starve.

Henry had been this way ever since he was born on this island that the wind was taking away as he lay there not sleeping. Wondering how old he really was, he thought of the island as it used to be when he was a boy, the two stores stocking shoelaces and bolts of colored cloth, the old hospital and the post office with over fifty boxes in the walls, little glass windows Henry would peek through and pretend he was looking right inside something mysterious—the innards of some complicated machine, some smart so-and-so's brain—like he was being offered a sneak at the way things worked in this life. And then the wind took that life away before he could put what he saw to any good use, and then the wind took Sarah and now what it was was him and the sisters holding out for the final storm to take them off island.

Because sleep would not come to Henry he got up and pulled on his waders and packed himself some bologna biscuits and a can of syrupy peaches like he liked and he boiled up last night's coffee and poured it in his thermos and took his flashlight out to search the weeds in front of the house for the stub of a Sweet he might have thought he'd finished one day when he was cigar flush. The beam sent sandcrabs sideways into their holes and Henry let the light play over the marsh wishing he could follow them down underneath the island where the wind could not get to them. Y'all be around way after I'm gone, he said to the crabs. Y'all wait, y'all still be here when this house is nothing but some rusty nails in the sand. He imagined his crabs crouched just belowground, ready to spring right back out once he switched his light off and give up on trying to find something to smoke himself awake good, imagined their big pop eyes staring right at him now, maybe their ears poked up listening to this sad old man out talking to the island like it cared to listen. He imagined the crabs calling to each other, hole to hole, old Henry Thornton won't never change.

What does it mean to change, Henry wondered as he cranked his outboard and throttled slow through the inlet toward the sound. What do I want over there across the water in nineteen hundred and eighty bad enough to give up whatever it is they're wanting me to give up? He'd spent the late sixties in Norfolk and all around him everybody was carrying on, army off fighting someplace he'd never heard of before or since, white boys growing their hair out and putting all kinds of mess down their throats, black people, his own children, trying to act all African, bushing their hair out and taking new names. Then crazies popping out the windows of tall buildings shooting presidents and preachers and the whole country catching afire. Henry brought Sarah home to stay. She tried to tell him wasn't anywhere safe left in this world, but Henry said he favored wind over flame, he'd rather be blown out to sea than die choking inside some highsky building with a brick lawn and blue lights streaking the night instead of the sleepy sweep of the lighthouse which he'd long ago learned to set his breath to.

Checking on the first of his crab pots, Henry told himself that Whaley said all that mess about him too old to change but was really talking about herself. Her sister, too. What had the two of them done to change but choose to remain on this island where there weren't any bananas on sale, nor nineteen-cent-a-pound fryers, buy one, get half off the other? He knew Sarah, had she lived, would have left him sooner or later, would have given up trying to talk him off island and gotten fed up with Whaley's ill mouth and Miss Maggie drunkstumbling across the creek to interrupt her Al Green tapes with a whole bunch of Where's Henry at, I need to ask Henry something, call Henry for me. Henry let the rope slide slowly through his hands, watched the empty pot disappear into the deep and cut the engine. He knew he would have let Sarah go, would have stayed on just like he was doing, providing for the sisters, getting hurt over not much of nothing, spending half his days just waiting on that wind—the last one, the big one that would take the three of them out of this life where everybody was waiting on you to change.

Henry knew this, too: if he went first, like they claimed men were likely to do, the sisters would have to leave. No way they could stay without him. Whaley could hurt him with her meanness, Miss Maggie could keep right on trying to get him to slip his hands somewhere they'd as soon not be, but neither of them could get on for more than a week without him. Without Henry there wasn't any island. Hell, I am that island, Henry said. Sarah when she passed cut me right in half. There's a side of me sits and smokes me a Sweet and just plain hurts, there's another part of me keeps the three of us and this island from blowing away.

Peering back on his island, Henry saw sudden movement behind the smudgy glass of the windows in the post office, a commotion he understood to be his big old secret come to him after all these years to let him know he knew something after all about this life. He fiddled with the locks on the windows, opened them right up and stuck his hand inside and wiggled his fingers around in that secret inside. It felt like something familiar, warm, his toes in wet sand or the slick of bait as he hooked a line. This life ain't blowed away right yet. I can sit right here in the sound and let the wind take me wherever and still make a change. He could lie back and eat a bologna biscuit and talk to Sarah and let the change come on ahead, let the skiff drift right across the sound to Morehead where he'd call Crawl and tell him, Crawl, you ain't won, don't think you changed me, I'm just here because the wind brung me over here and I let it. He could sit outside Crawl's yard and mend nets for the boys who still pulled things out of the sea, and he could think while he mended about the sisters and about how he'd saved them. Made them change. He could sit outside on Crawl's porch and smoke on a Sweet and close his eyes and know he'd go before the sisters but that he would not leave them on that island because here he was taking the island with him, right across the water, him and the wind. He could close his eyes and see the sisters sitting right up front at his funeral, sea-salty tears raining down on the Sunday dresses they had not worn for years. Hoarse preacher shouting out some Bible and Sarah whispering right over him how she could surely forgive Henry for not taking her off island before it was time for him to change. All eleven of his children and their children and the babies of his grandbabies looking up at the casket where Henry had laid down one day halfway through his crab pots, let the wind take him off island. Inside that casket Henry was sipping peach syrup and wishing he had one last Sweet. The sun was high and it was a mean sun. The church was crowded and so hot the air-conditioning was sweating and coughing like some sick somebody. Preacher called out a hymn. Let it be Sarah's smooth-as-liver singer sending me off sweetly. The sun and the water blended in brightness, the casket drifted, the wind picked up, the whole church rose up in song. Then came a lady in white passing out fans only to the ones who were moaning: sisters, hurting like Henry hurt, but thankful to be spared the wind.

Go Ugly Early

THE BRUNETTE SAID, "I prefer a man who can hold his liquor," so I turned my attention to the dirty blonde. She was big-hipped and slightly breasted, but her eyes were the blue-green of bottle glass and I liked the slinky way she swayed on her barstool.

"Hey, slobberpuss," she said to me.

"Oh, so you mind also that I've had a couple?"

"Do we feel discriminated against?" She was patting me on the head with her voice. "Are we just about to file a lawsuit?"

"We *are* in a bar. It's not like Quaker meeting."

"Oh, so like what did I expect? Do I understand that to be your point?" Her tone rose, shrilly.

"I'd say you and me are about even," I told her.

The brunette rolled her eyes and chewed her straw, searching the bar for me a few drinks ago. Hannibal could have just as easily come up against those Alps, said to his elephants, Fuck it, boys, let's don't and say we did. Would that Hitler had only found a little encouragement for his mediocre watercolors. All I'm saying is, history is nothing but a record of near misses, of last-minute left turns. Wars and religious intolerance and a source of potable water might have led people to settle in a cesspool like Gaithersburg, Maryland, which is where—in a happy-hour hotel lounge—I met my green-eyed Jessica, but I would wager large that the majority of settlers ran out of gas, steam, or money going north, south, east, or west.

"In what sense are we equals?" asked Jessica.

"*Now* who's toasted? I said *even,* not equals."

"Only slightly less offensive," said the brunette. Her name was Annie. Over the years she became a ghostly presence in a casually snapped photograph of Our First Night, sometimes a tourist passing blurry in the background, caught unaware in a frame of our nascent courtship, other times Mount Rushmore or the Grand Canyon, the attraction that drew us together. I suppose Jessica took the former view and I, mostly, the latter, as it was Annie, lithe and tall and wet-lipped, who drew me to that corner of the bar in the first place. Less of a head start at McCool's Public House down the street and my Jessica might be the one whose last name, thirty years down the rocky road, we might sit around the dinner table struggling to remember.

"In what sense are we even?" Jess asked me.

I thought of the old Churchill anecdote, about the woman at the dinner party who, disgusted by Churchill's inebriation, said, "Mr. Churchill, you're drunk," to whom he reputedly replied, "Yes, madam, but in the morning I will be sober, while you will still be ugly." I am not proud to report that this was what I was thinking, nor do I now believe it. Jessica is not ugly at all, I never would have married her if I'd thought so, though next to Annie and in the unreliable light of a couple whiskys and more than a couple Natural Lights, she did, I have to admit (and this is a record of honesty, as you will see I spare nothing here, especially as relates to my own failings) pale considerably.

I did not say what I was thinking that first night, of course. Nor did I answer her question, really. What I meant by it was, you seem as lonely and desperate as me, sweet thing. I meant, let's skip the sparring and call the round.

"Even Steven," I said with much drunken swagger.

Annie looked around me to catch Jess's eye, and they shared a laugh, which I recognized to be squarely at my expense.

"He's so articulate," said Annie, as if glibness were what she and Jess had come there to find. Of course I disliked her for rejecting me. I was about to suggest she adopt a strategy employed by some of my then friends: "Go ugly early, beat the rush" was their motto when they ventured, as we often did back then, to the dive bars and discos of DC and environs, in search of some short-lived companionship. Holding out for perfection would wrinkle and embitter her, not only that night back in 1977 but for the rest of her days. Sure, she was beautiful, but like most aloof beauties, she had an aura of detachment that made her seem not only unattainable but unpleasant.

Jess was more my style, though I can't say I was 100 percent certain that Jess was the one I wanted to spend my life with. To know beyond doubt—especially something that calls upon the notoriously fickle faculties of emotion—is more than highly suspect to me. I confessed to her my reservations—I could not have gone through with it had I not at least alerted her to the question in my mind—but I don't really think she heard me, and if she had similar doubts she did not admit to them. Something must have occurred to allow me to move forward. I remember thinking, Well, how could you be sure? We're talking life sentence here. Anyone who tells you they're completely sure is either of limited intelligence or lying.

We settled in Gaithersburg, Jess and I. I found a job writing press releases for the EPA and Jessica starting teaching eighth-grade science. We had two boys. They're both in college now. I don't watch them too closely when they're home on break, for frankly I don't want to know what they're up to nights. I know how we were, how *I* was, and it makes me glad I have sons instead of daughters. Sean and Frankie are good kids, we raised them to take responsibility for their own actions, and neither of them to my knowledge has ever been arrested, a claim I could not myself make at that tender age, but it really doesn't matter how well rounded and polite and self-assured they seem, does it? No doubt they pile into cars and cruise the dance clubs in search of willing females. No doubt they have their own slogans along the lines of "Go ugly early." (Perhaps that phrase is still in circulation.) Sometimes I grow despondent when I consider the great divide between thought and action, between word and intent. The way boys think of girls, the way we treat them before we accept the fact that we need them hugely: I do not like to think of my sons in that light.

We need them hugely. This is what I tell myself when I wonder, as I occasionally (if guiltily) do, how I managed to end up with Jess. The twelve-steppers are entirely right to suggest that we take one day at a time. Love, too, seems to survive best if parceled out in manageable increments. Of course it is not advisable to say to Jess, Baby I love you right now, in the car on the way to the grocery store, but as for what happens

when we arrive at Safeway, well, we're better off not specu-
lating. Though I confess if Jess said to me, David, I love you
today, but tomorrow isn't here yet, I would fully understand.
I am trying to talk now about the nature of love. Most men
just accept its mysteries in the way that they accept without
question the mystical properties of religion, jazz, baseball.
But I am trying to talk honestly about it. It is enough for Jess
to love me in the baking goods and school supplies aisle. It
would, I'm sure, be a comfort to know that you had enough
love to say, retire on, like money salted away in the bank. But
circumstances crop up to drain away your savings. Same, I
suppose, with love. You may have deep pockets, love left over
and lying idly around, and then something happens to siphon
it off.

What happened: We were in the Safeway, in the baking
goods and school supplies aisle, when someone—a woman—said Jess's name. She was tall and striking and vaguely
familiar. I assumed she was someone Jess knew from school.
It was early April, finally warm out, and she wore linen pants
in the manner of elegant but slightly down-to-earth middle-
aged women and a blue tank top. I moved a little farther
down the aisle, pretended to search for something as Jess often gets into interminable chin-wags in public, and though I
routinely accompany her when she shops (she claims to hate
to do it alone and it seems the least I can do), I don't relish

spending hours socializing in stores or parking lots. I was far enough away to comfortably sneak looks at this woman and not have my vision of her bare shoulders—toned and improbably tanned—ruined by the things that might have come out of her mouth. (Mundane conversation is such a turnoff. I can be attracted to a woman in passing for her physique alone, but a connection requires above-the-neck skills.) She was facing me and was a good four inches taller than my wife, and at one point she looked my way and caught me staring at her, and the way she looked at me without smiling, half appraisal and half dismissal, and the way her eyes shifted back to Jess and her face lit up at something Jess was telling her, took me back twenty-eight years to that hotel lounge. I was swamped by a wave equal parts lust and anger, a kind of combination I had not felt in years, the sort of emotion I did not want to think about my boys entertaining as they made their forays into the skirmish between the sexes. Still, I felt it in the Safeway. I was fifty-three years old, gray-templed and twenty pounds heavier than when I'd seen her last. My chest felt tight, my stomach roiled, my forehead grew hot. I allowed myself to acknowledge what I had so long denied: Annie and I were meant to be.

I grabbed a bag of flour and studied its ingredients when Jess brought Annie over.

"Guess who this is, David."

I held the box against my chest and gave Annie what I'm sure was a forced grin. The more you try to appear casual, the stiffer you become. See any posed photo for proof. Yet I needed to transmit to her the extent of my suppressed but still-vibrant desire.

I said, playing dumb, "Hi, I'm David."

She said hi, then added, "Ann."

Jess said, "Don't you remember Annie? She was with me the night we met."

"Oh," I said, and I tried, as I'm wont to do when nervous, to make a joke. "You mean in that sleazy meat market?"

Jess laughed her short, harsh, that's-not-funny-David laugh. I recognized it the way you hear a car alarm bleating in a blocks-away parking lot and know it's yours.

"Not too sleazy for me, of course," I said, trying to regain my footing.

"Too sleazy for us, obviously," said Jess. Annie smiled at this, and I remembered the way, that night, Annie and Jess had shared these conspiratorial smiles, and I realized that my life was a sham, that I had only taken Jess home to make Annie jealous, that Annie really wanted me that night, and her aloofness was proof that she wanted me still.

"Have you been living here the whole time?" I asked Annie. Jess had lost touch with her during that first year we dated.

I'd pushed her to stay in touch, but she gave up almost all her old friends when she met me. She did end up inviting Annie to the wedding, and Annie RSVPed that she'd love to come, but now her no-show made perfect sense.

"I just moved back here to take care of my mom."

"She's been in New York all this time," said Jess.

She wasn't wearing a ring. Jess would know her story. I wouldn't even have to ask; she'd spill it as soon as we said good-bye.

Which she did, after getting Annie's number, promising to have her over for dinner. She told me that Annie was divorced, had no children, had worked for many years as the office manager of an antiques broker, was widely traveled, had moved back to the area to take care of her ailing mother, was living in a town house down in Silver Spring.

"You found all that out while we were standing there?"

"I'm very efficient."

"So how many times has she been divorced?"

"She just said she was divorced. So once, I guess."

"She could have been divorced more than once, though."

"You never liked her, did you?"

It sometimes seems that life—or all our human interrelationships—can boil down to single questions, which the careless answer recklessly. I was driving, and I stalled as long as I could by studying the rear and side view mirrors as if our safety were suddenly imperiled. It was, of course, but not by anything outside of Jess's minivan.

I twisted around to check behind me before changing lanes.

"You know your car has a whopping blind spot," I said.

"You just never drive it."

"It's there whether I'm driving it or not."

"But I'm used to it. I know to look."

"I'm just looking out for your safety, baby."

"You didn't, did you?"

"Do what?"

"Annie. You never liked her."

I turned off the parkway into the neighborhood. If I said no, I never really liked her, chances were that Jess would arrange to see her away from the house. I'd see her only rarely if ever, not because Jess wants to spare me from those friends of hers with whom I have some problem but because she doesn't have to listen to me complain. She knows it's not worth it. She knows I can maybe keep my mouth shut, but keeping my mouth shut doesn't mean I rise above it. When I'm around someone I have problems with, my frustrations come out in gestures and expression and posture and even gait: Jess claims I walk differently.

If, on the other hand, I said I liked her, Jess might see fit to bring her over to the house a lot, which would suit me fine except the more Annie was exposed to the both of us, as a couple (insofar as we behave like a couple, however couples behave), the less likely she'd be inclined to act on her long-smoldering desire.

"I don't really know the woman," I said. "It's been over twenty-five years since I've even laid eyes on her. I was only around her a half-dozen times. Seems to me you guys drifted apart right after we started dating."

"Mostly what Annie and I did together was go out," said Jess.

"To sleazy bars?" I said. We were in the driveway, unloading groceries.

"That wasn't funny, by the way."

"It wasn't meant to be funny. It was true. That bar was sleazy."

"Of course it was meant to be funny. When you don't know what to say to people you try to make jokes."

"It's called breaking the ice."

"Okay," said Jess. I started to unload the bags, but she sent me out to fetch the rest. "We'll finish this conversation later," she said.

Of course, we didn't literally finish the conversation, though our marriage is characterized by conversations truncated and carried on wordlessly. Perhaps every marriage is this way: You have a disagreement, one party clams up for the sake of peace, but the argument looms in corners and edges. Layers of unfinished business pile up so that everything—a dresser drawer left open, the click of a television remote—seems an embodiment of the impossible task of squaring two fiercely separate realities. I don't buy the notion of marriage—or any sort of love—as the merging of souls. I merge into traffic on the interstate, but I don't become one with the tractor trailer belching black gas behind me. Sure, I can get outside myself long enough to put my needs on hold, but I can't check out of my own skin to inhabit Jess's or anyone else's, for that matter. Man might not be an island, as the poet claimed, but we all receive, at birth, our very own zip code. The beauty of this life: we all get to govern our very own municipality.

Jess met Annie—or Ann, as she seemed to want to be called—for lunch a couple of times during the next three months. I pumped Jess for as much information as I could, but Jess wasn't very forthcoming about these lunches and it wasn't like I could come right out and ask the things I wanted to know. It moved glacially, but I couldn't very well ask Jess to invite Annie over to the house without arousing suspicion. Besides, I had grown used to the slow burn of my life. It took years for any significant change to take place. There were things I wanted to change, but my ambition was suppressed by the dreary catalog of daily things that could, if not distract, occupy me, and I would look up and another year had passed, and I would accept the pace of my life, however dilatory, as my own.

Five months after we ran into her at the grocery store, Annie showed up at the house for drinks. When Jess told me that morning she was coming, I said, "Why'd you invite her over for drinks? Drinks is something you usually reserve for people you aren't sure about. Like neighbors or coworkers you don't want to spend a whole evening with."

Jess was just back from the Y, dressed in spandex from some sort of class, aerobics, Pilates, I could not keep them straight. To be frank, she'd been working out three or four times a week for the past ten years and I could not see much of a difference to look at her. Middle age had settled weight around her hips, which was hard to hide. I'm heavier myself, and don't get nearly the exercise I need, but what woman expects a middle-aged man to have a flat stomach?

"Honestly? There's something sort of cold about Annie. It's like she's not quite there. Maybe it's just that we haven't seen each other in forever and we're different people now. At least I hope I'm a different person now than that night when I met you. Anyway, I just can't seem to be able to connect with her the way I used to."

I made a noise—"huh"—which of course she translated into a paragraph or two.

"What? You think I never should have started up with her again in the first place? That was then, this is now? Or, I forgot, you never liked her, did you."

"All I said was huh, Jess."

"Meaning?"

"Meaning what time is she coming?"

We had drinks on the deck. Our neighborhood is old for Gaithersburg, so much of which exploded into repetitive cul-de-sac suburbia in the seventies, but that evening, looking across the neighbor's lawns at their ugly metal storage sheds, their concrete birdbaths and aboveground pools, I saw our place through the eyes of someone who had lived for years in Manhattan. What losers we must be to her, having stayed here in the place where we met. Everything in our lives seemed shabby or fourth rate. The clothes we wore. The cheap plastic stackable lawn chairs I'd bought from Home Depot. The wine we drank.

I don't know what Annie and Jess were talking about because I wasn't listening. I was watching Annie talk, studying her eyes, her arms, her long lovely legs. Her coldness, her distant attitude toward Jess, had been all the proof I needed. It was obvious on the deck how she was physically present but emotionally elsewhere. *Clipped* would be the word to describe her conversation. We talked about Gaithersburg, for God's sake. People she and Jess used to know. I mostly sat there sipping bad wine and every once in a while tossing in an ironic comment.

She left after two glasses of plonk.

"See what I mean?" said Jess.

"Well, okay, she's kind of hard to talk to. But I think it's important to hold on to friends from ages ago. I mean, I wish I'd done that. I just burned through people. I don't keep in touch with anyone from high school or college or my old single hound-dog days."

"So why should I?"

"Because you have the opportunity. I haven't run into anyone in the grocery store that I used to be best friends with."

"They have telephones, I'm sure."

"Not the same at all. It's awkward, calling someone up after twenty years. Much better to run into them on the street."

"She exhausts me. Also, I think she's a snob."

"Why? Because she lived in New York for so long? There are lots of unsophisticated idiots in New York, you know."

"She's neither unsophisticated nor an idiot. She's just like up above everything."

"She'll come down to earth once she gets comfortable

again. It must be hard for her, coming back here to take care of her mother after all those years away. Is she seeing anyone?"

"How should I know? We talk but we don't really talk. She's never really ventured anything about her private life, and I certainly got the feeling that it was not something I ought to ask about."

This bit of information warmed my belly like a shot of whisky, radiating its heat outward through my veins until it reached my heart. Everything fit. All I had to do was figure out how to get her alone.

I should say here that I had never, in the twenty-eight years we'd been together, strayed from Jess. Despite my early bar-hopping, hoping-to-get-lucky days, I need to connect deeply with a woman, intellectually as well as physically, before I can truly engage. I've not felt that with anyone besides Jess. I don't think I ever considered that I'd fallen out of love with Jess when Annie came back into my life. It's just that Annie touched parts of me I had not felt in so many years, and I figured she was put there to bring those long-dormant parts of me back into play. I even considered the notion that it would be good for my marriage to have some passion reintroduced into my life.

Annie's number was in the Rolodex, so a couple weeks after she came over for drinks I made my move. I told Jess I had business in the city after work, and I called Annie from my office around five thirty. She didn't seem surprised to hear from me—her voice was as arid and distant as always. I'd rehearsed a half-dozen dialogues, most of which involved Jess wanting me to drop something off—which I was counting on Annie recognizing right off as a ruse—but what if I was misreading the signals? What if she hung up the phone and called Jess immediately to thank her? Every reason I could come up with, every excuse, seemed shot all to hell with holes. In the end I decided to have a little faith. I called her up and told her I was in town late and would she like to meet me for a drink.

"Okay," she said. "Where?"

I named a bar I knew in Bethesda.

"When?"

It seemed she'd been waiting for my call.

A half hour later we sat in a dark corner of an Irish pub, drinking Pinot Grigio. I confess the conversation was halted and awkward for the first five minutes at least.

"I wanted to see you alone," I said after a torturous silence.

Her iciness had not melted, but she smirked a little at this, which I took as a good sign.

"I wonder why," she said.

"You know why."

"Tell me why, David."

"I've always wanted you. Since that night."

"Well, I can see why."

"What do you mean?"

"Married to her."

"Jess is her name."

"Right. I knew her before you did, remember. She's just as annoying now as she was back when we used to hang out together."

"So why did you hang out with her, then?"

Annie shrugged. "Seemed like the right idea at the time. Plus she always drove. And when I was too broke to go out, which was often, she always offered to pay. She had the means. But of course you know that."

It was true. Jess's father's family owned much of what became the commercial strip of Gaithersburg. They'd been hand-to-mouth farmers only a generation before, and then the exurbs spread north from the city and the cornfields formerly farmed by Jess's forebears became strip malls with names like Oakfield Crossing and the Shoppes at Cornwallis Creek. We would never really have to worry about money, though this is not at all why I married my wife. I said as much to Annie.

"Why did you marry her, then?"

I twirled the stem of my wineglass around on the napkin.

It seemed that sleeping with Annie would be far less of a betrayal than the next words out of my mouth.

"Why are you here?" I said.

"Because you asked me to come, silly." She'd warmed up a bit, seemed almost flirtatious, but I didn't like the way she looked at me. "Anyway, I asked you a question first."

"Why did I marry her?"

"That's the question."

"Can we go back to your place?"

"If we're going anywhere, we're going to get a hotel room. But first I want you to answer my question."

"Why do you care? It would seem to me that the last thing you'd be interested in talking about would be Jess."

"Well, you're wrong. What I'm interested in is how you could fall for someone so boring. Not to mention stay with her for, how long has it been?"

"Twenty-eight years."

"How many of your wife's friends have you met in town for a drink during the last twenty-eight years?"

"None. You're the only one."

She didn't need to speak, as her laugh let me know how bad a liar she thought I was.

"We can go get a room when you answer my question."

"This is absurd, Annie," I said.

"I go by Ann now. I have gone by Ann for years. But you don't want to accept that either, do you? You want it all to be like it was twenty-eight years ago, when we were all too young and dumb to know what we were doing to each other."

I thought of my sons in a bar, minutes from last call, furiously chatting up the last two available girls, wondering how they'd let it get this late. All their friends had scored, were off in strange bedrooms or out in the parking lot, in steamy backseats. Jess at home fixing my dinner, listening to *All Things Considered* as she sipped her single glass of Chardonnay, still dressed in her workout clothes.

"You were supposed to fuck her, not marry her," said Annie. "Wasn't that the plan? What went wrong, Dave?"

"I love her."

"You were a lonely little boy who needed his mommy to cook his dinner."

"She's right about you. You're wretched."

"Well, I'm happy to hear that," said Annie. "That actually makes me like her. She deserves to think ill of me. I fully admit my faults. In fact, I've never tried to hide them. I prefer people to be up front about such things. I do hate a phony."

"So what are you doing here?"

She shrugged and finished her wine. "This is the sort of thing I do."

I called for the check.

"You'll be going home now, I guess."

"You'll be giving Jess a call, I guess."

She reached for her purse and slid out of the booth. "I guess you're in enough trouble already."

I sat there until the waiter brought the check. He was so overly courteous to me that I imagined he'd been spying on us from the bar, had seen the whole thing, and was commiserating as only a fellow soldier could.

"That one got away," I said, forcing a smile.

"She was a beauty, that's for sure," he said, and his own smile was just as forced, but then he whistled, and it was the most grating and intolerable noise I've ever heard in my life, that whistle out of the waiter's mouth.

I Will Clean Your Attic

AFTER HE LEFT HER it began to snow. The house was huge and drafty without him, its rooms silent and overly bright in the new whiteness. This was the South, and snow down south brings its own brand of frenzied incompetency. There is no budget for salt and sand; the main thoroughfares are ineptly freed of drifts but the side streets are left marooned. The schools shut down at the first sign of flakes and stay closed until grass once again dominates the soiled slush. Stores surge with overtime stock boys and delivery trucks but lose the fight to the flood of anxious customers who line up for bread and beer and candles.

To Laura it was only snow, and she knew it would not last. She found things to like about it: Children squealed and tumbled outside, and birds lingered with gratitude in the box of feed outside the breakfast nook. Music sounded alive in the firelit living room.

And yet it was intolerable, for it made all the more painful Christopher's absence. It turned rooms hollow, the snow. As it lingered she closed the curtains and paced, entombed. The mail stopped coming. A note appeared in the slot: *Unable to deliver, ice on steps.* She looked forward to catalogs with the indifferent intensity she paid to cooking shows. She neither ordered merchandise nor cooked more than rice and the occasional chicken breast, but without her distractions she felt desperate. Before the snow came, three weeks after he left her, she had just been able to sleep again, four-hour stretches uninterrupted by nightmare or the angry punching of numbers on the phone. She had managed a movie, a workout in the pool; she spent a weekend preparing her tax return. But now everything was buried beneath the bright layer that made teenagers polite and distant neighbors friendly.

When Saturday arrived, she forced herself into an ancient down jacket Christopher had left behind and stuffed her sweatpants into boots and went out to the garage for the snow shovel and the rock salt and went to work on the front steps. One thing at a time. She had avoided therapists for she knew what they would say and why go to the doctor when you save yourself the money and drink the prescribed fluids and rest and take the necessary steps on your own? No one else was going to help her out of this. Cleaning the steps was not going to help her. Small mindless tasks were rumored to help and she forced herself to chip away at the ice to spite the therapists she did not allow herself to see, as if to say, See there? I did it and it did not help.

The front door had been shut tight and locked for a week now, and the lock was frozen. She struggled to open it, her boots sliding on the wood floor. There was no traction; she pulled the edge of the rug over and tried again and finally it swung free. A slip of photocopied paper, a flyer, drifted inside. Its edges had curled, its print had faded, as if it had gotten wet, then dry, then wet again. She could barely make it out. I will clean your attic. I will shovel your walk. *I will I will I will*—a long list of *I will*s, domestic and household chores. The refrain suggested the writer had been ordered by a teacher to write one thousand times on the blackboard his litany of *I will*s. I will not give this any more attention than thou would a pizza coupon, she vowed. But she studied it, the cold rushing in from outdoors, her limbs starting to shiver as she read it over and over. A name—B. R. Bradshaw—a phone number. She folded it in eighths and stuck it in the pocket of her husband's abandoned jacket. Let him deal with it. Though it was never his job, she always spent more time on the yard than he did. She took care of the house and yard and he took care of himself. He needed to be taken care of and while she took care of home and him he found a woman named Sydney to take not necessarily better but a different kind of care of him, and sometimes, even though she knew it wasn't true (for she had heard Sydney's chirpy whispering once on the phone when she'd picked up by mistake), she found herself wishing Sydney was a man. At least if Sydney was a he, Christopher might miss the kind of intimacy that a woman could give a man. She wasn't so much shocked by this thought as bored by it. She had had even more pathetic thoughts and now she was simply exhausted by the bathos.

It took all afternoon to clean the steps of ice. The next day at the regular time for her mail to come she read at a book in the living room, paying more attention to the sound of the postman's approach, the rusty slot opening, the plop of newsprint and envelope on the floor, than the book in her hand. But he was late. And when she finally picked up the paper, something less demanding to read while not reading, she discovered it was Sunday, no mail.

And then it was Monday, then Wednesday, and the mail fanned out on the floor where it had landed and she found herself ignoring it. If the absence of catalogs was so painful, she was better without them. She told herself this. She told herself a lot of things, over and over, mumbling them aloud as if learning a new language in preparation for departure to a country where she knew no one.

The mail she heaped on the coffee table. For a week it grew until one day it toppled. She bent to clean the mess from the rug and discovered yet another flyer from the attic cleaner. B. R. Bradshaw. Perfect name for a workman. Didn't they all go by their initials? She pictured his pickup in the drive, aslant from bad tires, its dashboard adrift in receipts and more of the same crudely executed flyers and empty cigarette packs. She sat in the corner of the living room studying the flyer.

She went to work at the free clinic, interviewed prospective patients, forced herself to believe that their misery was real. The flyers kept coming. She threw them away, she pulled them out of the trash and kept them in a stack. Determined to stop the flow, she dialed the number in a rage one day, her breath coming hard and hot as the dial tone bleated. The voice on the answering machine was the generic computer-generated voice of some woman who sounded, in her electronic monotone, slightly British. Laura had owned one of these herself once, cheapest on the market, so cheap you could not personalize your message. She hung up in horror, as if she'd called back in time to leave herself a message. Don't marry him, her message would say. He will clean your fucking attic.

One Saturday she read the long afternoon away in the living room when the doorbell rang. She shuddered at its echo, bolted up as if someone was spying on her, as if this was not her house and the owner had come home to surprise her squatting there. A year or so ago, the house had been broken into while they were out at a party; since Christopher left, she'd been nervous, especially about opening the door to strangers. She crouched on the sofa, peered through the blinds. The man on the stoop looked both suspicious and familiar. Like someone she'd interviewed at the clinic. She did not want to open her door to him until she realized that she had probably sat across from him in her office. She had never once had a patient show up at her house and was too curious to ignore the bell.

He introduced himself. B. R. Bradshaw. She knew she should cut him off before he got started on his attic-cleaning spiel, but she found herself embarrassingly eager to check him out. He was a few years younger than her, late twenties maybe.

"I run a small business. Odd jobs around the house. You should have gotten my flyer, I sent a couple your way."

Laura realized that she'd never seen a postmark.

"Sent? You mean you mailed them?"

"Well, no ma'am. I dropped one in your box, I was working your neighborhood."

"With a vengeance," she said.

"What's that?"

She was glad he did not call her ma'am again.

"I got more than one."

"Haven't had a whole lot of takers. Lots of people don't want to think about spring cleaning right yet."

"Spring cleaning," she said. She wanted it to be a question. She wanted to consider it as an option, something she ought to have thought of herself now that the season of Christopher's abandonment had passed and a natural division had been reached, an organic and easily observable one of weather and calendar.

"I do attics, garages. I'll do your basement."

"I don't have an attic," she said.

He cocked his head and looked at her. He backed down the walk and cocked his head again, at the house this time, looking up at each side, stroking the stubble on his chin, posing all the while as if he was being asked to improvise a mood in a drama class. Exaggerated incredulity. She studied the attic cleaner's eyes, milky blue, stunning against the blackness of his unfashionable shaggy hair. She watched him pantomime suspicion and when he walked back to the stoop she said, "Okay, I have an attic. What is this? You go around trying to catch people in lies?"

He laughed. "I don't imagine there'd be much profit in that."

She wanted to laugh also, but she was a little uneasy at how heartlessly she found herself mocking this guy. B. R. Bradshaw. She heard herself on the phone to a friend, "I got a guy who can handle that for you, B. R. Bradshaw, no I'm not joking, I know, isn't it perfect? "

"So look," he was saying, "if you say you don't have an attic I guess that means you don't want it cleaned."

"Come back later," she said. But why? She didn't want him to.

"Attic out of town?"

"Gone south for the winter," she said.

"Condo in Florida I guess."

"Actually, Mexico. A cabana."

She wanted him to leave but she had fallen into a rhythm and she was enjoying it, and she realized that this was the first time she'd engaged in such spontaneous and meaningless chatter since Christopher left.

"I guess I'm like my neighbors," she said. "Not quite ready for spring yet."

He shrugged. Bony shoulders rising beneath the too-large Lehigh sweatshirt.

"It'll come. Before you know it, it'll be summer."

She shrugged herself. A shrug seemed the only appropriate response to the passing of seasons she did not have the strength to heed.

"But you aren't like your neighbors," she heard him say.

She braced herself for a cheesy come-on. She sort of hoped he would, so she would not feel guilty for not wanting to open the door to him. Then she could tell all her friends, the ones who'd lost patience with her moping, the ones she knew were tired of listening to how much she loved Christopher still and hated him, how badly she wanted to forget about him and how easily she'd take him back this minute, now, no questions asked, about this creepy guy, and get extended credit in the sympathy department.

"Your neighbors don't even answer the door."

"Maybe they didn't care to be blanketed by flyers."

"Blanket? That bad?"

"You hit pretty hard."

"I want work bad enough to be persistent I guess."

"Come back next Saturday." When he was gone she realized this was exactly the way she dealt with Christopher, too. Oh, so you found someone else, okay, go away and come back when you feel like it. Next Saturday maybe? She went back to the sofa and her book but found herself instead of reading dreading the Saturdays to come in this life.

But one came, a week later. She thought of disappearing, going out of town, but she knew he would turn up again. He was a blanketer, persistent, he wanted work.

"What'll it be?" he said.

She looked out in the drive. "Don't you have a car?"

"I'm on foot today," he said, "but if you need something hauled off I can run get the truck."

She stared at him long enough to let him see her skepticism.

"I didn't know what you wanted me to do for you today."

"Clean my attic, I guess."

"Okay if I put the stuff out in the garage, come by and pick it up later?"

"How did you know I have a garage?" It wasn't visible from the front of the house at all—it was not really a garage, but a listing shed in the far right corner of the yard.

"When you didn't answer the front door I figured you used the back," he said. "I tried the back door once, back when we had that big snow."

She didn't like the thought of him sneaking around, disliked even more his boot prints in the snow she tried so hard to keep virgin. It had become a game during the days before the snow melted, seeing how little she could disturb the whiteness with footprints, making sure only her own tracks led in and out of the house that was hers alone now.

"Let's get going," she said.

He followed her in. The phone rang when they were halfway up the stairs. She told him to wait, but he kept climbing. "No problem," he said. "I'll find it, it has to be at the top of the house."

"No, wait here," she said. Alerted by her tone, he froze on the steps while she raced to the kitchen, her face tight at the thought of him sneaking around upstairs, checking out her bedroom.

"You sound tired," said Christopher.

She was sick of people telling her she looked tired, or sad, or thin.

"I can't talk now," she said. "What do you want?"

"Can you talk or can't you?"

"Fuck off," she said, and hung up.

She took the phone with her, sure that he would call back. Usually she wanted him to, usually she told him to fuck off so he *would* call back, but halfway to the stairs she returned to the kitchen and cradled the phone and switched the machine on. Since he left she'd not used it; she hated to come home and hear the glee in his voice when he'd called knowing she was out and thus avoided talking to her.

"All set?" said B. R. Something in his voice suggested he'd overheard her phone conversation. She passed him on the landing and led him into the guest room closet from which a staircase led to the attic. They stood among the piles of boxes and suitcases, the framed diplomas and the guitar cases.

"For someone who doesn't have an attic, yours is in bad need of cleaning."

"You know, you might want to think about branching out." She felt she still held the phone in her hand, her every nerve poised for its shrill trembling.

He looked blankly her way.

"You're kind of overly specialized, don't you think?"

"You trying to tell me attics don't need cleaning?"

"Seems like the kind of thing most people would want to do for themselves."

"Kind of personal, hey?"

She looked around at the junk. Mostly Christopher's. She didn't like B. R. Bradshaw's tone, which suggested he knew more than he let on.

"Hey, look, doesn't matter to me what it is. I'm not cataloging, I'm toting."

She laughed. The word *tote* always made her laugh. "So tote that barge lift that bail," she said.

"Tell me which one to lift and which to tote and I'm there."

She pointed to a set of free weights, told him to take them down to the garage. It was a three-trip job, and while he was gone she went about organizing piles of Christopher's belongings she wanted out of the house. Almost all of it was his, and though he'd taken his clothes, he'd left most of his stuff here and she wanted him to, for it meant that once he tired of the girl named Sydney he would be back. I'm not leaving you for her, he'd told her time and again, and every time she'd asked him why he was with her, he'd said, I'm not *with* her. I see her sometimes, but it's not like you think. Nothing's like I think, she thought. The world is not what I think, it's what you think and always has been, your reality was the one we moved around in and now you have a new one and it's not some place I'm dying to visit. He'd wanted to see her, to have dinner a couple times a week and go to movies and even take an occasional trip together, springing for separate rooms but holding hands in the car, on walks at the beach. *The only thing that has changed is that I just can't be with you right now. I need to be by myself. I love you as much as I ever have, baby, I just can't be with you right now.*

"You have no idea how much you've hurt me," she said to herself as he lugged his mother's hook rug to the pile.

"What's that?" said B. R.

She hadn't heard him come up.

"What does B. R. stand for?" she asked.

"Ben Randolph."

"Not Benjamin Randolph?"

"Just Ben."

"Why not go by Ben?"

"Just never have," he said. He seemed shy now. She saw that he'd rather ask questions than answer them.

"Would you like something to drink?" she asked.

"That would be nice," he said. "But I ought to get all this down first." He pointed to the piles. The garage had no door and she knew she should not leave Christopher's stuff out in the open, since they'd been broken into before, and even if nothing was stolen a storm could blow rain in and ruin everything. Yet she'd already started this attic cleaning. She'd hired herself an attic cleaner.

When he finished she heard his knock at the back door. She offered him a beer.

"No thanks. Never touch it."

"Never?" She didn't know what she'd do without a drink at the end of the day. She knew she was drinking too much in the eyes of, say, her grandmother or her family doctor, but she never had a hangover and never drank before six and she felt she had full license to, if not drown her misery, bathe it a bit each night.

"Oh, I used to."

She felt bad for pushing, but he didn't seem at all bothered. In fact, it seemed he wanted to talk, despite his earlier reserve when she'd asked about his name.

"I quit going on seven months ago. Six months, twenty three months in fact."

She got him a Coke from the refrigerator and tried to change the subject, for it seemed too much like her job, listening to the testimonies of the recently rehabbed. He was talking about his Alcoholics Anonymous meetings, and though she considered herself a compassionate person, she had an unwarranted and unfair distrust of self-help of any kind, especially those groups that seemed to her Sunday school dressed up in street clothes. She half-listened as he described his home group, how often he attended meetings, his sponsor who was helping him now with step 9.

"What's step 9?" She didn't want to be rude. It was hard to enjoy the beer she'd poured into a fluted schooner, but she could not simply ignore him.

"Step 9's about making restitution to the ones you've hurt."

"And who are you making restitution to?" Before the words were across the table she realized how nosy she sounded. She had the childish urge to put her hand over her mouth. She thought so constantly and obsessively of Christopher now that communion with others, on any other topic, felt impossible.

"You," he said.

She put down her beer. "No, really," she said, and he interrupted her to say, "I'm serious, Miss..." and in the silence she realized he was waiting for her to say her name, which she did not want to say even though she would write him a check soon enough and he would know.

"What are you talking about?"

"You had a break-in back a couple years ago."

As she felt the blood rush to her face, Laura put her hand around the glass of beer.

"That was you?"

He tried to look penitent, which made her even angrier.

"Get out," she said.

He held up his hands. "I'm not here to ..."

"I don't care what you're here to do. You're not here to clean my attic, that's for sure."

"Really, if you'll tell me your name so I won't have to keep calling you ma'am."

"You stole my husband's checks. You know my name."

"That was a long time ago. Maybe you kept your name when you married him. For all I know you're not even married anymore."

She stood and reached for the phone. "I'm calling the police."

"Won't you at least let me apologize? I just came here to make amends, I wasn't planning on charging you for ..."

"Oh, so you're going to make up the price of the stuff you took? Let's see, some silver, a CD player, a VCR, a television, my husband's checkbook. What about the less tangible things you took from us? The safety, the peace of mind, the happiness. You think you can pay that back also?"

"I'm sorry," he said. "You're crying, don't cry."

She started dialing. He was gone by the time the 911 operator came on.

"Just forget it," she said, and hung up.

She drank the rest of her beer in a swallow and poured another, took it into the living room. Drinking, she remembered the night of the break-in, the party they'd gone to, one of Christopher's coworkers, an obligatory affair with all the canned laughter and dead silences and salted peanuts of office parties. She'd drunk too much jug wine. She barely remembered the ride home, tense and stiff, as if she'd carried the forced conviviality away on her clothes. In the car she criticized a woman Christopher worked with for no better reason than her cocktail chitchat was tedious. As if her own at these affairs was quotable. Christopher had started in on her then, her ambiguous statements interpreted, her judgments examined.

They'd fought their way inside and carried on their fight in the kitchen and the creepiest part of that night was this: they did not realize someone had been there until the next morning. They'd gone to bed still angry, Christopher turning away from her to read, she too tipsy to read curling wine-groggy and anxious into a fitful night's tossing. The next morning, when Christopher went down to make coffee, he'd noticed the spaces where their possessions had been, discovered the missing CD player, the silver pilfered from a bottom cabinet, a week or two later his checks missing from a file cabinet in his study. She did not care in the least about losing these things; what bothered her was how they could have settled down to their miserable sleep in a house violated, how they could have ignored it, not felt it, another presence in the sanctity they'd managed to preserve during the roughest of times. She realized later that despite the tension of that night, the way they'd both gone to sleep still angry, they—at least she—had pretended an invincibility no longer possible. She'd assumed it would all be fine in the morning. In memory the burglary seemed the beginning of the end.

The day after she ran B. R. Bradshaw off, Laura had an alarm system installed. It took the better part of the week, as she opted for the type that activated each window, the most expensive system available. She called her lawyer to see if there was some way Christopher might share the cost of this extravagance, as it was his defection that made the purchase necessary.

"I'm good, Laura, but I'm not that good."

"It's his fault," she said.

"Maybe you should have checked with me before you had it installed."

"I still need it whether he pays or not," she said. She thought of telling her lawyer the story of B. R. Bradshaw, but so far she had told no one, which was strange—she remembered half-hoping he might hit on her that first day so that she might use his advance to garner sympathy from her pity-depleted friends. But it did not feel right, sharing this secret with any-one else. And it seemed more powerful if kept a secret, even from Christopher, though the thought had occurred to her that if he knew he might even come home. Perhaps this in-cident would remind him of the vow he took. She'd never thought to take it seriously herself when they were content, but now it seemed a monumental promise. Love, honor, pro-tect. If the greatest of these was love, she'd settle for the least of these, the last.

Twice during the next week she set off the alarm acci-dentally and had to apologize to the sullen dispatcher at the police department. The junk from the attic remained in the garage, a reminder of many things—the return of the bur-glar to the scene of the crime, Christopher's leaving, a cleaner attic, the coming of spring. She liked looking at it out the kitchen window at dusk, a bourbon warming her stomach, fueling her indignation at the way things were.

On Saturday evening she heard a noise at the back porch. Immediately afterward the alarm went off, and she grabbed the phone and ran to the kitchen to find Christopher at the door, his keys in hand, his face screwed into a wince at the bleating of the alarm. She tried not to smile as she held up her hand to signal for him to wait, called the police department to explain that it was an accident, switched the alarm off, and stepped out on the back porch.

"Jesus, Laura."

Laura shrugged. She looked behind him to the shiny Volkswagen Jetta in the drive. Christopher wore gym clothes, and was sweating. Before he left the most exercise he managed was a walk around the block.

"New image, new car?"

"It's Sydney's. Mine's in the shop. Speaking of new toys."

"You forget we were broken into. I live here by myself. I need to feel safe."

She regretted saying this, as it suggested to him that she'd felt safe when he was around, but he seemed too flustered at setting off the alarm to pay much attention.

"I came to get some things out of the attic."

"You might have called."

"I did, remember? You told me to fuck off and hung up on me."

"I had it cleaned," she said, and when he looked confused she added, "The attic."

"What do you mean you had it cleaned?"

She didn't answer, for she thought she had given it away, her secret, her attic cleaner.

"I mean I cleaned out the attic."

"You got rid of my things?"

She crossed her arms and nodded at the garage.

"Oh great," he said. "You get an alarm for your stuff and you leave mine out for the taking."

"You want it, take it. I don't think anything's missing."

"I'll have to rent a truck."

"I know a guy who has a truck. He'll deliver it. He's pretty cheap."

"Who?"

"You don't know him."

"I don't think that's such a good idea, do you? I don't send Sydney over here to pick up my mail."

She couldn't decide whether to laugh or slap him. It amused her, Christopher assuming the housebreaker was her Sydney, and it infuriated her that he thought her capable of replacing him in a few weeks' time with some guy who owned a truck.

"Some of us find it hard to go from one lover to the next without even stopping to take a shower."

Christopher said, "Well, who is he then?"

She thought she heard a bit of jealousy in his voice. Maybe I should have played along, she thought, but what's the point of stooping? Besides, she wouldn't exactly win when Ben Randolph showed up in his janitor pants. Christopher would only feel sorry for her. She wouldn't mind pity from her friends, but she was strong enough suddenly not to need it from him.

"He's just some workman. I hired him to do some yard-work."

Christopher looked around the yard.

"He hasn't started yet," she said.

He sighed and turned to look at the garage. "Okay," he said. "When?"

"Next Saturday."

"You're going to leave it out here for a whole week?"

"Take what you can. Unless Sydney's particular about her car."

"Why do you insist on making this harder?"

"Because you do?" she said, and she left him there on the porch. From the kitchen window she watched him haul a few boxes to the trunk of the Volkswagen before giving up and driving off. Before he'd even backed out of the drive she was on the phone to B. R. She felt oddly elated calling him, as if it could not wait another second, and was disappointed when the monotonal British lady came on to ask her to leave a message.

That week she succumbed to leaving her own machine on when she was at work in case B. R. called. She'd asked him to call if he had any questions, otherwise she'd see him Saturday morning, but she'd assumed he'd call to let her know he was coming anyway, and found herself a little disappointed at night when she came home to no blinks on the machine. It wasn't until late Friday night, sitting up at the kitchen table with a cooking magazine and a bottle of Zinfandel, that she realized she was anticipating his arrival as she would a date. But he wasn't a date, he was a thief. She wondered if he'd been watching the house for some time, if in his surveillance he had learned things about them that they didn't know, or care to acknowledge, themselves. Perhaps he was more than just a garden-variety thief; perhaps he was expert at reading the subtleties of the homes he violated, choosing to break and enter into only those homes that were already broken.

Oh, come on, she told herself as she corked the bottle and rinsed out her glass so she would not have to come upon the red dregs staining the glass in the morning, he's just some brainwashed dry drunk who wants my forgiveness. Having someone ask her forgiveness seemed luxurious to her, no matter that it was the wrong party doing the asking.

Early the next morning—an hour before she planned to get up—she heard a car in the drive and looked out of her window to see him already out of the truck, crossing the yard to the garage. She took a twenty-minute shower, which did not succeed in washing away the bleariness. She'd been overserved, and she told herself it was a weekend, but still she felt guilty, as if he would take one look at her and know that she stayed up late with a bottle. She knew how reformed drinkers could turn sanctimonious about everyone else's drinking habits. Like divorced people she knew who became suddenly and implausibly knowledgeable about other people's marriages, as if they could sense from a tense word or brusque gesture everything that was hidden from view.

He was far too chipper, and she told him so.

He laughed. "Used to I'd be getting home about this time. Though most weekends I didn't bother going home at all. Now I have a meeting I go to every morning. Dawn Patrol. Start the day out strong."

She offered coffee, but he declined, saying it would take several trips and he had other work to do that afternoon. She tried not to show her disappointment.

"Where am I taking it anyway?"

"I'll have to ride with you, I'm awful at directions."

He put the box he'd grabbed down on the tailgate of the truck. "You sure?"

"You don't allow passengers in your truck?"

"I just thought, you know."

"What?"

"Well, that you hired me to do it because you didn't want to do it yourself."

"I'm not going to help you unload it. I'm just going to navigate."

"Okay," he said, but she could see from his expression that it was not okay, that he did not approve. She went in for more coffee and a doughnut from the carton she'd bought at the store the night before to share with him. Why do I need his approval? she thought, going teary at the kitchen sink. He's the one that needs something from me. Still, when the truck was almost loaded she poured him a glass of juice, took the doughnuts out to the back stoop, and was pleased when he sat down to eat.

"Is it hard for you, not drinking?"

He chewed for a while, swallowed. He did not look at her.

"You think about it all the time. You know that feeling you

get when you leave the house to go to work or on a trip and you realize you might have left the stove on, and you can't rest until you go back and check it out?"

She nodded, unable to speak. She knew that feeling well these days. She would manage a few seconds of distraction, or blissful freedom from thoughts of Christopher, and then her not-yet-believable circumstance would crop up to antagonize her. It had not gotten the least bit better so far, and it had already been three months.

She knew a little something about denying something you loved. But what was a bottle compared with a heart you cannot imagine living without? Who was he to go around claiming to be maimed, when it was only corn, barley, hops, and sugar he was battling, rather than heartbreak, misery, loneliness unto cooking shows?

"I used to imagine what my life would be like without booze," he said, reaching for another doughnut. "I'd even have dreams, or visions, of what it would be. Clean white sheets on my bed. A good shave every morning."

He caught her stealing a glance at his cheeks and blushed.

"I thought everything would be in control, you know. That everybody I hurt would take me right back, and when I'd come around they'd be glad to see me. I figured I would never again have to stick my hand between couch cushions in my sister's den searching for dropped quarters. I thought maybe I'd be able to stay with a woman longer than a few months. Fresh start, clean slate, second chance."

Laura tried hard to listen but found herself thinking of how she'd imagined her life without Christopher, of the deep loneliness and misery she'd envisioned, which had turned out to be true. So she was better off than this attic cleaner. At least there were no ravaged expectations. Her imagination had not swindled her.

"I take it things aren't perfect yet."

He turned away from her. "Let's just say I'm a whole lot better off than I was."

"Let's go," she said. She went inside to put away the doughnuts and find her wallet. She did not think she was a whole lot better off than she was before, she did not want to be better off than she was before, she wanted her husband back and yet she knew that he wasn't coming back. And she knew also that the home B. R. Bradshaw violated was already violated, that she could not blame him or herself or even Christopher for the dissolution. It may have seemed like snow down south—she might have pretended to be caught unprepared, ill equipped to handle the cleanup—but the disturbance had been brewing for some time, and she'd done nothing to take shelter.

In the truck she gave directions to get them out of the city, then lost herself in bitterness until she looked up to find him scrutinizing her.

"Which way now?" he asked.

They were stopped at a light at the edge of the clustering strip malls that ringed the city. She knew only vaguely where she was going. Several times some years ago, when they were remodeling their house, she'd gone to the landfill with Christopher, but he'd always driven and once they got out of town into the country, the side roads all looked alike to her. She didn't want to ask, but he would know soon enough where they were going.

"You know the way to the landfill don't you?"

He tapped the brakes and turned to her. "You're taking all this stuff to the dump?"

"I don't need it anymore. The dump is where you take stuff you don't need, right?"

"If it's something that no one else might need, sure. But there are other places to take perfectly good merchandise."

"The same place you took our CD player, right? And my grandmother's silver? But not my husband's checks, I guess."

"Your husband left you, didn't he?"

"Just drive."

"You're dumping his stuff to get back at him."

"Look," she said, "I don't need this from you. I hired you to haul this stuff away, not to counsel me."

"You don't really want to do this, you know."

"You don't really know what I want. What do you really want from me? You want my forgiveness? Is that all?"

"I don't expect you to forgive me. It's just a part of my recovery, making amends to the parties I've wronged. I don't have a lot of say over a whole lot in this life, like whether you forgive me or not."

"So all you have to do is apologize, and then it's fresh start, clean slate, second chance?"

He pulled off the road then, into the parking lot of an antiques store. She tried to focus on the things the owner had put outside to entice customers, but the rickety office chairs and mediocre oil paintings depressed her, as they reminded her of the load in the back of the pickup, which would soon be dumped among the hills of ordinary daily waste. Christopher's cross-country skis and the leaky pup tent where they'd survived a freak April snowstorm in Linville Gorge, left for scavengers to find.

"What is it you want me to help you do?" he asked softly. "Because I know it's more than just clean your attic."

She started to cry. She looked away from him, at an older man in a rocking chair on the porch of the store. He wore oversize black shades favored by people with cataracts, but she could tell by the way he cocked his head in their direction, his gaze frozen on the bed of the pickup, that he was interested in their load.

"Look, it's okay," he said when she did not answer him.

"No, it's not okay," she said. "I'm not ready to forgive anyone. I'm not capable of it, and I don't see why I should have to go around forgiving everyone their sins. It's not what I'd imagined for myself, this bitter old martyr I've become. I might as well open up a confession booth in the mall. Make some money out of it at least. I can quit my job and slurp Icee's behind the curtain and dispense forgiveness to the wretched all day long."

"Maybe you need to forgive yourself."

She turned to face him, felt the heat in her cheeks, turned away again. The antiques dealer was still studying the merchandise. "For what?" she said to the dealer, although she was talking to her attic cleaner.

"I couldn't really tell you what for. But it seems like to me you're being awful hard on yourself. Blaming yourself for things that aren't your fault."

"That's the problem with you people," she said. "You refuse to take responsibility for your actions. Don't blame yourself, blame someone else. Blame your genes, blame your parents, blame suburbia. If I blame myself it's because I'm brave enough to accept the blame."

"Okay," he said. Simply, softly: okay. She waited for him to continue, but he left it at okay, as if they had come to some agreement. As if it was okay by him if she accepted the blame.

They sat there. The engine ticked, and the cab of the truck began to heat up. She wanted to roll down the window, but she did not want to draw the attention of the antiques dealer.

"That guy over there's already got his calculator out," said B. R.

"Yeah, I noticed. I don't have any antiques, though."

"Just old stuff you want to get rid of? I bet he'd take it."

She looked at him again, carefully this time. He was wearing a cap, and his hair was wild beneath it, and his eyes were kind even if she did not want to trust them.

"Where does he live?" he said. "I'll drop you off at home and take it over there."

Why not? she thought. She could squint and pretend he was Christopher, come back to retrieve his things, or she could look him dead in the eye and forgive him, this housebreaker who, no matter what he'd taken from them, had at least forced her to clean her attic.

"I guess we can call it even now," she told him, even though she knew, and suspected he knew as well, that both of them were a long way from finding any kind of balance. She felt the load shift in the bed behind her as he whipped the truck around in the parking lot, and when a box toppled onto the gravel and he braked to retrieve it, Laura angled the rearview so that she might watch it shrink and told him to keep going.

Muddy Water, Turn to Wine

JESUS HAD JUST LEFT Chicago, bound for New Orleans, when the girl beneath James stopped moving. Lit by dancing candlelight, she cocked her head as if she heard something over the second cut of side 1 of ZZ Top's *Tres Hombres,* an album James would never have expected a girl to choose as sound track for a little late-night, bars-just-closed coupling. The walk from the bar to her garage apartment through the charged quiet of dark neighborhood streets, the way she laid him down on the tightly made bed while she went about lighting the half-dozen windowsill candles, the sound of the vinyl slipped from its sleeve and soon after of the arm falling, the needle scratching, the first bass-heavy notes of an album from James's youth: James thought maybe he might be in love.

He did not hear the phone ringing. He kept up with Jesus, who was working from one end to another and all points in between. *Aw, take me with you Jesus,* sang ZZ Top. James was working his way down the Mississippi, *muddy water turned to wine,* when he finally noticed that Erin, beneath him, had stopped somewhere south of Chicago.

She had not gone rigid, as she might had there been someone in the room with them; she'd slackened a little, rocked gradually to a stop. Her eyes were wet. James heard the gurgling phone. It seemed to be buried under a towel. Boyfriend calling, he surmised. He knew squat-all about a boyfriend, but then he knew squat-all about Erin except that she'd just started waiting tables at the restaurant where he washed dishes and she was a music theory major and she was big-boned sexy, and over the fall and winter James had shed twenty-two pounds. At five ten, 137 pounds, he now favored flesh. He knew nothing about any boyfriend because he assumed it was her job to declare such a thing and it wasn't something he'd ever think to ask of a girl who'd invited him back to her garage apartment after twenty minutes of making out on the muddy lawn of He's Not Here, any more than he'd have thought to ask after any communicable diseases. Neither yesses were likely to make his night, which back then, late summer 1981, was about as far as his headlights shone in the dark.

"Do you need to get that?" He regretted these words as soon as they escaped, thought they sounded annoyed, clichéd, or both.

"I guess," she said, but the phone rang three more times, muffled but persistent, before she made an effort to slide out from under him.

He watched her fish the phone from beneath the drift of clothes they'd peeled away and stretch the cord so that it reached into the bathroom. Of course she would do this— whoever called at 3 a.m. would likely require privacy. But it hurt a little. Or maybe he wanted it to hurt. He conjured a flash of jealousy or, rather, of bruised affection, which perhaps he could maneuver to sleep with her again.

She was gone for so long that James flipped the album. ZZ Top sang about a whorehouse in a Texas town called La Grange, where they had a lot of nice girls. *Just let me know if you wanna go.* James lit a cigarette from a candle, thumped ash into the bottom of his cowboy boot and, when Erin did not return after five minutes, figured he ought to just take off.

He was stretched across the sheets, reaching for his jeans, when the bathroom door opened, and then stopping to crank the music up so loud the window glass hummed, she had pinned him sideways across the bed. He pulled Erin down to him and while kissing her silently promised never to leave.

Afterward, the uneven candlelight made his temples hurt. He wanted another beer. He said, "There's just something about a garage apartment."

"What do you mean?"

"Yeah, I don't know, I mean, they have this aura. Sort of romantic, sort of tree-housey?"

Erin got up and went to the bathroom, leaving James alone to consider his desperate appraisal of garage apartments. When she returned he lifted the covers up for her, but she stood above him, biting a fingernail on her left hand. Her right arm dangled. James could see that her mouth was twisted, as if she were sucking on her lip to keep from saying something.

"My dad died," she said.

"Oh, wow. I'm sorry."

"That was his wife on the phone."

James sat up. "Wait, you mean *now*? He *just* died?"

"You think they'll be okay at work with me taking a few days off?"

"Of course," said James. He reached out for her hand, the useless one, but she stared at the wall above his head. He could not say why, but he felt like he'd remember that arm, the way it hung, forever.

"Man oh man. When's the funeral?"

"Monday, I guess."

James tried to remember what day it was. It was summer, he went out every night after work, everyone did, you closed the restaurant and then went to a bar or to someone's house, no real reason to know the day of the week. He knew he had the weekend off. After a few minutes he figured out it was Thursday night, technically early Friday morning.

"How will you get there? I mean, will someone come and get you?"

Erin said she guessed so. She said it so morosely—as if having to be fetched for her father's funeral were the saddest part of all this—that James, because he knew she did not have a car (she rode a pea green, wide-tired Schwinn with a milk crate wired to the handlebars; he'd used the bike as something trivial to talk about when he'd moved down the bar after work and took the stool next to her), said, "Well, I could take you."

"That's crazy," she said. Because she had to, he knew. You *have* to say certain things, especially to people you just slept with. But she never once commented on the prominence of his rib cage, on the way his jeans drooped off his ass, his belt wrenched way past factory holes, buckled into ones he'd punched himself, crudely, with a screwdriver. She did not mention the sharpness of his hip bones, which could easily bruise anyone who came even wondrously into contact with them. She did not ask if he was sick. James was thankful enough not to want her to repeat the things that rote lovers awkwardly repeat.

"Why is it crazy?"

"You have to work?"

"Nah, I'm off this weekend."

"I'm sure you had plans."

She wasn't crying. She seemed a little distracted but not terribly upset. Maybe she was in shock. He thought about the way she'd come bounding back to bed after getting off the phone with her dead dad's wife (not, obviously, her mother; not even her stepmother), how she stopped to crank the music up, the things they'd done to each other before she said to him, My dad died.

"I can cancel them," he said.

"They weren't all that big?"

Now she was making fun of him. This was good—at least she'd veered from the script—but it was also, well, weird. Though he wanted to tell her that his ode to garage apartments was sincere, that he could love her just as much for where she lived and how she traveled to and from her cluttered, candlelit tree house—pea green, wide-tired Schwinn—than any of the more common and less interesting reasons people clung to. He wanted to say, Let's just not go through all that this time. Let's just up and skip it.

"They were medium."

She laughed out loud at this, which did not make him uneasy as he attributed it to nerves.

"Just let me take you," he said.

"You don't even know where my dad lives."

"I figure you'll let me know once we get on the road."

She mentioned a town on the coast.

"Just let me go home and get some stuff together."

"In a minute," she said, lifting the covers and sliding in close and warm next to him.

BACK AT THE HOUSE James shared with friends from his student days, evidence of a late night cluttered the porch, the living room, the kitchen. An unidentified boy lay cocooned in a sleeping bag on the couch, dirty blond bed head, cushion-roughened cheeks, his mouth opened as if his jaw, in sleep, had come unhinged. Noticing the sweat on the boy's brow, James shook his head in halfhearted disgust, went into the kitchen to make a thermos of coffee for the road. Out the window, a water tower bearing the insignia of the university rose in silhouette against gray sky above the trees, reminding James of his own father, angry at James for not finishing his degree.

Listening to the coffee drip, James decided to call and cancel, then a second later wondered if, just in case she asked him to stay, he ought to pack his interview suit. He'd have to stuff it behind the truck's seat so she would not see it. He whispered some things to himself in time to the dripping coffee: Just let me know if you want to go. Let's up and skip all that.

As she climbed into the truck he studied her face for signs that she'd been crying. She appeared both exhausted and organized. She'd brought her bicycle, asked if he could tie it down in the bed so that it would not slide around.

"I don't want to have to depend on people to take me everywhere while I'm down there."

James nodded, though he wondered, Will she ride her bike to the funeral? He pictured black limousines, a line of old southern lady Buick 225s, her green Schwinn sandwiched between them. He added it to the list: garage apartments, *Tres Hombres,* rides her fat-tired beach bike in the funeral procession.

He wasn't comfortable with the silence that overtook them out on the highway. He told her twice she could sleep if she wanted, but she just rooted through his tape box, ignoring the weepy acoustic side of James's personality, the Joni Mitchell and the Dylan and the Leonard Cohen for louder, raunchier choices: Lou Reed's *Rock N Roll Animal,* a Mott the Hoople album he only played once a year. Maybe she was trying to keep herself from sliding into despair. He kept quiet until they hit the flat, sandy tobacco fields southeast of Raleigh. The low roadside swamps made his ankles itch, made him anxious.

"Well, the seventies are over," he said.

She had one foot on the seat, the arm holding her cigarette elbowed on a knee. He noticed it was the same arm that had appeared so forlorn hours earlier.

"Yeah, like a year ago," she said.

"Taking a while to sink in, I guess."

She rolled her eyes and appeared to wince.

"I mean, aren't you glad?" James said.

"Why should I be glad?"

James shrugged. "It just seems like we got gypped. I mean, the sixties were crazy and all this important shit went down and on either side are these really gray decades where basically nothing happened."

Her laughter was so sharp-edged that he decided to pretend to be joking. "You know?" he said.

"I don't know what you're talking about. I don't think about time like that."

"How do you think about time?"

"Certainly not in decades. It's like you're scared you're going to be tested or something. You sound like a history major."

"Sociology."

"But you dropped out, right?"

"I'm going back next semester," he lied.

"I might have to take some time off myself now," she said. He assumed she meant because of her dad.

James said, "Listen, if you want to talk about it."

"About what?"

"You know, your dad and all."

"I imagine I've got plenty of talking about it ahead of me. Can we stop and get something to drink?"

"Of course," said James. He took the next exit and pulled into the rutted lot of a low wooden store. Inside, the bowed floor creaked. The air smelled of something at once rank and sweet. Brutal late-morning sun poured through faint rectangles on the plate glass, the ghosts, James guessed, of posters announcing church bazaars and turkey shoots. In the back they hesitated by the drink cooler, which buzzed in a way that suggested its inefficiency. He started to make a joke about it, but her father had just died.

Erin slid open the door and grabbed a six of Tuborg Gold. She must have noticed the look on his face because she said, loudly, "You want anything?"

He shrugged and reached for his own six-pack. After all, he had no mourners to greet, no funeral to attend. He followed Erin to the front of the store, but halfway to the register she stopped at a bin and fished out a pair of thick-soled orange flip-flops.

"What size shoe do you wear?" she asked him.

He did not tell her that he could not wear flip-flops, that they hurt his feet.

"Eleven," he said, and she grabbed a gray pair. At the register she told the clerk, "I'm paying for his beer, too."

When he protested, neither Erin nor the clerk looked his way. He was aware of his skin-and-boneness, self-conscious about his cheekbones, the way the word *emaciated* seemed to pop into people's vocabulary the minute he showed up.

"Y'all have a nice trip," said the cashier as he handed Erin her change. Back in the truck, James realized that it was just like a trip to the beach. The music she chose, the way she kept her window open and surfed the breeze with her hand, the beer, the way she sat with a bottle between her legs, her flip-flopped feet on the dash, her knees against her chest, eyes hidden behind her shades. Yet she'd suffered the kind of loss they say you never get over. James had never had anything happen to him, really. Well, he'd flunked out of school. He'd shed twenty-two pounds. What caused it was not a mysterious illness but this crazy love. He'd loved this girl so hugely that he'd lost all his friends over it. She'd been gone a year and his roommates had just recently started treating him the way they had before he'd met her. A week after she left, she wrote him a letter that said *I would die for you,* and two weeks after that she moved in with some guy she knew from her English class and would not answer his phone calls. When he called her up at her job, she treated him as if he was harassing her. "Whatever happened to I would die for you?" he said to the dial tone after she hung up on him. At the time, James thought it was the worst thing that would ever happen to him, but sometimes it seemed nothing more than someone saying what they felt at the time.

"You're not wearing your flip-flops," she said to him.

"I would die for you," said James.

These were the words that came to him, and so he said them, aloud, on the way to Erin's father's funeral. He wasn't sure why—because this was what he felt at the time? He'd damn near been ruined by something someone said to him that she felt at the time, and this wasn't even the worst of what he'd just done. Bringing up dying at a time like this?

Erin looked over at him, her eyes slitted behind her shades. Then she looked the other way, out the window, and drained her beer, and opened another.

"I'm sorry," said James, "I meant . . ."

"No, don't," she said. "Don't talk. Just put on the flip-flops I bought for you."

He steered with his knees in order to slip off his sneakers and socks. When he had the flip-flops on she reached across and patted him on the knee, as if to say, There now, all better.

• • •

THEY'D EACH HAD three beers when the air began to smell of sea. They hadn't been talking. Erin had cranked up *Sticky Fingers* and they'd sung a warbly duet to "Wild Horses."

Her town announced itself in fits of fish camp and motor court.

"Tell me where to turn," he said.

"Take the beach road," she said. "I want to get wet."

"I mean, aren't they expecting you?"

"I'm always late," she said.

She wasn't lying. She'd been late to work twice and had only been working there a couple of weeks. In fact, Monroe, the manager, had told one of the other waitresses that Erin wasn't really working out. Now's my chance, James remembered thinking when he'd moved down the bar to ask her about her bicycle. It was only last night, but it seemed months ago. He wondered how long ago it seemed to her. She'd said she had a different concept of time. Plus—he had to keep reminding himself of this—her father had died. Trauma does strange things to the clock. When he'd been sick, when he'd done nothing but lie in bed and sweat, that intolerable stretch between late morning and three o'clock, when he could hear the school buses lumbering up and down the streets, the squeals of schoolchildren, the sounds of his housemates drifting in from class, had lasted days.

At the beach she directed him to a motel called the Atlantis.

"I assume you're staying the night at least?" she said.

"I haven't really thought that far ahead."

"I was under the impression that you had the next decade planned out."

"I mean, I guess I ought to hang around and sleep off the beer."

"You always start your sentences with 'I mean.' What do you mean?"

James swallowed. He felt unduly perturbed by her question, which after all was innocent enough. He got out of the truck without answering and slapped his way across the hot parking lot, the flip-flops sliding off his feet.

Inside the room he went to the bathroom and stayed there for a while, allowing her time to change into her suit. He knocked before he came back out—it seemed the right thing to do—but Erin, in answer, said, "Who's there?"

"I'm coming out," he said, and he heard her laughter, and then the door opened and she stepped naked into the bathroom and pushed him against the sink.

They lay in the sagging bed listening to Casey Kasem on the clock radio. She got up during a commercial and put on her suit. When James got up to join her, she said, "Do you mind if I go by myself?"

"Not at all," he said.

She stuffed her clothes into her backpack. "I'll just ride my bike home. It's just across the bridge, on the waterway."

"Oh, I don't mind dropping you off, I mean . . ."

"I know you mean everything you say," she said, and he remembered telling her he'd die for her, and he felt the itchy heat of shame prickling his skin, and he closed his eyes. When he opened them she was standing by the door staring at his bony torso. He knew she was wondering what was wrong with him. He could tell she wanted to ask.

"Okay, well," he said. "Hey, I'll be around if you want to drop by."

James got up and fished the extra key from the pocket of his jeans.

"I'm not going back till tomorrow sometime, I mean, I know you'll be busy with your family and all but . . ."

"I'll see you later, then," she said, and she was gone.

He woke hours later to the sound of her key in the lock. It was dark out, the room lit only by streetlights strained through drapery, and James heard car radios, shouts, the night noises of beach towns. He was hungry and his head throbbed. He asked Erin what time it was, asked if she slept—after all, they'd been up for more than twenty-four hours before she left for her swim—but she did not answer him. She was stripping off her clothes and then she was alongside him in bed.

Maybe it was fatigue, or perhaps it was patience, even compassion—his desire for her to get what she needed, to provide
her with some fleeting bliss in this difficult time—but James
lasted forever. They kept at it for well over an hour. It wasn't
the most satisfying love James had ever made, but it was different from anything he'd experienced. More physical, less
self-conscious. It wasn't violent or rough, but there was a force
beneath their movements, a purpose far beyond the kind of
pleasurable distraction from his problems that had led him
to take a seat next to her on the barstool and, a couple hours
later, stumble up the stairs to the garage apartment.

In time he figured it out: She wasn't there. She was trying
to show up. Beneath him was only vapor, only her aggressive need to materialize. It was not desire, really—at least not
desire for him—but it wasn't desperation, either. Somewhere
between the two. It left him feeling weightless. Weightless-
ness was not something he needed to feel. He cataloged what
usually motivated the friction of lovers—desire, vanity, ego,
athleticism. Love, fifth and lonely on his list. He lay worrying
in her arms as she slept and realized, too late, that it had to
do with grief.

When he woke again she was gone. He put on his swimsuit
and went out to the beach, which was empty save for a few
older women seeking shells. James realized that it was Sun-

day, that he really should be leaving soon, but he couldn't very well leave without saying good-bye. He went for a quick swim and spent the rest of the day sitting by the pool, watching the room, scanning the beach road for her bike.

Near dark he called the restaurant and asked to speak to Brian, the line cook.

"Where you been, man?" said Brian. "I tried to find you last night, but your roommates said you disappeared."

"I'm down at the beach."

"Wish I was. Hey, that one chick's dad died."

"Which one chick?"

"The one you were talking to the other night. Where did y'all get to anyhow?"

"I walked her home."

"Yeah, well, her dad died. Least she said so. She's going to get canned, man."

"Because her dad died?"

"Monroe said he was going to fire her anyway."

"Why?"

"I guess because she sucks at waitressing? Plus, she's weird, right? Hey, aren't you supposed to open tomorrow? You better get your ass back up here, man, he'll fire you, too."

"Save him the trouble," said James. "Pick up my check for me, will you? I'll call you in a couple of days."

James hung up the phone and sat at the edge of the bed, considering his role. She needed a ride; he'd given her a ride. She needed him to be there, in bed, so that she could prove something to herself that he knew had nothing at all to do with him. Maybe it had little to do with her father's death. He thought of a term he'd heard his father, who sold insurance, use: a preexisting condition. We're all carrying around these preexisting conditions, James decided, which are irritated or soothed by the next thing we happen to come into contact with. The thing was, he wasn't sure if he was irritant to her, or salve. He only knew he felt purposeful enough to put on his interview suit and the gray flip-flops she gave him and wait for her return.

But she did not turn up for hours. Restless, James took a walk on the boardwalk. His interview suit was a couple of years old, bought when he was twenty pounds heavier; in the ocean breeze it flapped around him like a sail. James sweated in the light summer wool. He could smell his dress shirt, sour and yellowing around his armpits. The flip-flops hurt his feet, but he felt he wore exactly the right outfit for a man in his situation. The suit suggested compassion, sympathy, even commitment. As for the rubber shoes, well, he'd wear them until they blew out, as flip-flops inevitably did, and then he'd save them forever in a closet bottom, a reminder of the lightness of love, the low cost of its initial investment, the frivolity and giddiness of it even in the face of trauma and hardship.

In an oceanfront, open-air bar, James sat drinking orange juice in case the funeral was today. He did not want her to come for him and smell vodka on his breath. He angled his stool away from the view of the ocean, toward the boardwalk, so that he might see Erin if she came searching for him. The half drunks who came and went in groups, wearing bathing suits and T-shirts with the names of other beach bars, stared at him derisively. James wasn't bothered, as they all seemed so clueless, so uninitiated into this world he'd discovered through motives that were admittedly less than pure. Or were they? James faced the boardwalk, trying to decide if he was wrong to move down the bar that night, if this fullness he felt, this new purposefulness, were merely the result of chance, rather like a lottery, or if he had been *delivered* to Erin, if their respective needs—her grief, his illness—had magnetized them.

Well, what did it matter now? Here he was, at the beach, drinking orange juice as the sun set over the arcade facing him, redeeming in its final wash the very skin it had ravaged all day long on the faces and arms of the drunken boardwalk throngs. He decided just to trust this moment of sun, though he was out of work, low on funds, dressed like a homeless insane preacher.

Because they didn't hold funerals at night—at least James had never attended one—he motioned for the bartender to add a little vodka to the juice. All day long he'd been attracting drunks, who seemed drawn to his eccentric dress, as if anyone dressed this way at the beach had a story to tell. He'd waved them off until his third screwdriver, after which James found himself surrounded, slapping high fives with sweaty strangers, giving hugs to girls who went by their initials—B. J., T. J., even an O. J.—who wore bikini tops and cut-offs.

"Well, the seventies are over," said James.

"We're up to 1981, preacherman," said a squat black guy who had taught him an elaborate, multipart handshake. "You been on vacation?"

"I'm just saying, I'm glad to be shy of that decade. Aren't you?" he asked one of the bikini-topped girls.

"She just takes it one night at a time," said B. J. or T. J. about her friend, who smiled easily at everything James said, as if his attire made him seem unusually amusing.

It was late when he returned to the room. He was drunk enough not to notice Erin, curled up under the covers, the air-conditioning cranked high.

She was watching him undress. She laughed a little at the clumsy unknotting of his tie.

"Where've *you* been?" Her emphasis on the *you* suggested playfulness but underneath he detected need.

"I didn't catch the name of it," he said. "Everybody there seemed to go by their initials, though."

"That could be any place down here," she said. She reached for his hand and yanked. He fell across her, but she flipped him over and climbed on top. It wasn't as good as before. A problem surfaced with the rhythm; at first it felt syncopated, but soon it turned disastrous, like the ragged drumbeat of a high school marching band reverberating off buildings blocks away. James tried not to notice her frenzied eagerness to finish.

The sheets were soaked with sweat. They lay under the roar of the window unit. She appeared to be in oxygen debt. His own breathing was shallow and emphatic.

James, when he caught his breath, said, "Am I your lover?"

She said, "My dad did not die. He called me an irresponsible, spoiled rotten little bitch, though. He told me if I bounced another check he would see to it that I never got another penny from him as long as I live."

He put his face to her side and listened for her heartbeat but heard only the air-conditioning unit, struggling to keep them comfortable. He kissed her rib cage, thinking of those things he liked about her: garage apartment, beach bike, ZZ Top. After the girl he'd loved left him, James had stopped eating. He thought she'd see him and understand how hurt he was and come back. It took over a year and twenty-two wasted pounds—it took until this moment in the sticky darkness—for James to realize how hard it was to love a crazy person.

"I fucked up," she said.

"It's okay. People fuck up. Also, people die." He raised his head up, like a periscope. "I mean, you know that, right? Someday your dad's going to really die."

He felt the jolt of anger in her tightened muscles. "You said you'd die for me," she said. "What were you thinking?"

"I guess I was thinking that maybe, at that moment, it was sort of true."

She was silent. A different kind of silence from her—not sullen or bored, but rigid and anxious.

He got up to get dressed. In the dark, he found his way into his suit pants, his dress shirt. He stuffed his tie in his pocket and toed the gritty carpet in search of his flip-flops. A match scratched against a strike pad. She lit her cigarette and stared at him over the low flame.

"Okay, all right, you're my lover," she said to him.

"No," said James. "I'm just an overdressed tourist."

"There are worse things," she said.

"Not in a beach town. Listen, I'm sorry I said that about dying for you and all."

She smoked her cigarette. "I guess we're even. Being that we're even, do you want to get back in bed?"

He wanted to say that the seventies were over. But the seventies, or the end of them, meant nothing to her, and James understood that anything he said would be weighed against his one regrettable promise. He stood awkwardly by the door, knowing he had to say *something,* for despite what he'd whispered so many times in his head to the girl who had left him—*you can't just go around saying things*—James understood that was exactly what people did. They traded Chicago for New Orleans, muddy water for wine. They stood, like him, with their hand on the doorknob of a rented room, the air conditioner circulating words they fell back on like breath.

The Right to Remain

ON THE FIFTH PASS of the night, Sanderson pulled the car alongside the curb across the street from her house. He lit a cigarette, cracked his window. Focused his slitty eyes on the blinds in the neighbor's windows, dared them to peek between the dusty slats. What the hell you looking at? I can see you, but you can't see me.

Walter, riding shotgun, said, "Why we stopping?"

Sanderson stared past him at her house: a sprightly yellow bungalow he helped her move into the last time she'd left him. The previous owner had left a sculpture in the yard assembled from bicycle parts rearranged to create not a bicycle but an animal at once prehistoric and futuristic. It rose up in the tiny yard where Sanderson thought it better to plant a tree. He had never trusted it. He looked at it in disgust, then past it to the living-room window, dark save for a blinking visible in the back room where she slept. She kept the television on all the time now, he knew from the few disastrous times when he had broken down and called her. It gargled along in the background, a noise just white enough to compete with the buzz between his ears. There were pauses in her responses, when she bothered to respond to his questions at all, that suggested she was actually listening to prime-time television. The pauses lasted for years and were filled with the kind of impatience he felt when a fantasy of the two of them together again was interrupted by something trivial: a guy asking him for a light, a cashier naming the price of a purchase.

"Women always leave me in the winter," said Sanderson. He tossed his cigarette into a neighbor's yard and jerked the window up against the chill.

"Maybe you ought to move to a more southerly clime, chief," said Walter.

"I ought to send that fucker my gas bill is what I ought to do. Many miles as I've put on this car lately making my rounds, seeing if he's showed up yet. I ought to make him pay for an oil change at least."

"Make his ass pay is right," said Walter.

Sanderson said, "I knew a girl from New Orleans, she told me it gets cold down there. Real wet cold, too."

"There ain't no escape, is there?" said Walter. "You take your chances. It's a risk, every time you hook up. Like you're taking your life in your hands every time you unzip your drawers."

Sanderson started to point out that it was not exactly your life you took in your hands every time you unzipped your drawers. Instead of arguing with Walter, a thorough waste of his precious time, he let himself consider the old boy, seriously. Why had he asked him along to ride shotgun in the first place? He told himself that he did not want to be alone and that he thought having someone along for the ride, a witness, might prevent him from doing the things he woke up each morning having already done in his sleep.

But he and Walter were members of the same club—broken, bitter-hearted ex-lovers refusing to move right along. Walter's wife had left him, too, though Sanderson did not care much for that wife. Carolyn was her name, or was it Carol? He knew Walter from work, and Carol treated all of Walter's work pals like they were responsible for all the things Walter failed to do: come home on time, call when he was not going to come home on time, stop at the third drink, stop by the store on the way home from the bar for milk and diapers, make more money, lose some weight, make her feel that something special she had never felt with anyone else except some boy in high school she could never have snagged. Sanderson thought Walter was better off without the bitch, but he would never have told Walter so, because Walter's bitterness over losing her kept him on call for ridiculously necessary excursions like the present one.

"I know exactly what kind of car the motherfucker drives, too," said Sanderson, as if they had been talking about him the whole time.

"He's here?"

"Not yet. He'll show, though. Tonight's the night." Sanderson had to believe that tonight was the night, for he had this problem with timing. It was off in general, always had been. He'd been born this way, according to his mother, who had him in a hallway of the hospital. Chronically off kilter. The woman he loved used to make him feel so bad for it—she told him once that she left him because she was tired of waiting for him to do the things he claimed he was going to do.

"Hold up," said Walter. He reached in the side pocket of his bomber jacket and pulled out an envelope. It appeared to be some kind of bill, probably unpaid if he knew Walter.

"What?" said Sanderson.

"Little trick I learned from my own extensive tour of duty in the jungles of heartbreak," said Walter. "See, whenever you feeling like pulling something crazy, you write down exactly what you're about to do and why. Then you put it away for a while, come back to it when you're settled."

Sanderson thought this too pathetic to acknowledge. He wondered where a guy like Walter would pick up such a lame and useless tactic. He looked over at Walter, drawing lines on the back of his envelope, and wondered if the poor son of a bitch wasn't better off miserably married to Carol.

"We got two columns here," said Walter. "One's for the things you hold him responsible for. The other's what she done. You got to be able to separate the two."

"Why?"

"Because they're two separate things, man. Let's start with him."

Sanderson stared at the blinking coming from her bedroom for a long time before answering.

"What do I hold him responsible for?"

"Correct," said Walter. "Give me some ways he's screwed up your life. Go ahead and start with the obvious if I were you. Numero uno: he's boning the love of your days on this planet."

Sanderson rifled through the drift of bills and receipts on his dash for an open pack of cigarettes. "If it's okay with you, Walter," he said, "I'd rather work my way up to that one."

Walter shrugged. "Hey, it's your list. Maybe you're right. Start with the small stuff."

None of it was small to Sanderson. He made his list in his

head, silently, lovingly, and was not shocked to discover that he held the party in question responsible for crimes and misfortunes of many years.

1. Flunking out of college.
2. Two DUI's in the past five years.
3. Stupid feeling I have when I'm around my family at holidays and it seems like there's something I'm supposed to say to claim my kinship to them or make them understand who it is I am, but I don't know the right words and so they pretty much just ignore me. I open presents and eat turkey and get the hell out of there quick.
4. Acid reflux.
5. Failure to do much besides laugh and nod when guys at work like old Walter here start in talking shit about spades and homos.
6. Bottles. Bottles hidden away in crawl spaces and tire wells and toilet tanks of the houses where I used to live. Empties that if lined up in a row would run from Richmond to Shreveport. All the money I've wasted on drink and right now the tepid backwash in this bottle I hold in my hands and I blame you too for me liking this particular drink a whole lot better when there was a whole lot more in it.

And another thing: Surely he was the one who had handed Sanderson the coffee laced with bourbon on the night of the fire. Who better to dose him with the very medicine which caused her to leave Sanderson in the first place? He did not see a face, just a gloved hand holding out a Styrofoam cup with a little steam whistling out of the hole in the lid. Some stranger handing it over to him in a moment of need—this was the story he told anyway: that he drank it down in the shock of watching his porch cave in and by the time he realized what it was he was drinking, the alcohol bubbled in his bloodstream begging more. Too late by then, needed more to stave off the tremors, plus the stress from watching his house go up in smoke. His own brother, who had bailed him out of jail and picked him up off the floor of his kitchen and signed him into rehab three times said to his wife that night of the fire, Hell, let him have it, what else has the guy got now?

He thought about how easy it was, the fire. Leave the fire door open, the comforter close on the hearth. In his story to the fire chief he was lying on the floor by the fireplace, went out on the porch for more wood, wasn't gone but a second or two, and when he came in the comforter had caught fire to the couch, the whole room was smoke and then flames, he barely managed to get Coot, his dog, out of there alive.

Well, he did leave the room. That part of it was true. Left the edge of the comforter in the firebox and left the room to shoo Coot outside and when he came back he had the bottle he'd bought earlier in one hand and the cup of coffee, still hot from the drive-through, in the other.

"Well?" said Walter.

"Let's go with her first," said Sanderson after a pause.

"Whichever. Shoot."

But Sanderson made the same silent list. What he could not bring himself to say aloud was this: that she was making him feel like he had taken some medicine intended not for him but for someone who maybe gave a damn, and this medicine had acted on parts of him he did not know he had. For this he should be grateful?

Sanderson cranked the car, slid it into drive, eased away from the curb. His quiet, careful movements made the low idle of the Ford sound surreptitious. He felt like he was getting away with something until he remembered what he was letting her get away with.

"Let me think about it some while we drive," said Sanderson.

"Naw, man," said Walter. "Big mistake. Don't go thinking about it. You ain't done nothing but think about it night and day. Tell me about it, I been there, all I could think about was her. Ate slept and drank her for months. I tell you, it was hell."

"Carol left you for someone else?" Sanderson knew the answer to this: who would have Carol? She hung on to Walter long as she did for just that reason, because he was all she could get, and when she figured out he was just going to take whatever she gave him she left him.

"No," said Walter. Almost a whisper. "Won't nobody else."

"So you don't know what this is like, buddy."

"Well," Walter started. Sanderson looked over and down at him. He was slumped in the seat; the shoulder harness seemed the only thing keeping him from melting onto the floorboard. He appeared dejected, humiliated to be confronted with an aspect of suffering at which he was not expert. Kicked out of the club.

They were quiet all the way back to the bar. They chose a seat in the dark this time, way back by the jukebox. Away from Cynthia, a matrimonial near miss from Sanderson's younger, wilder days, who refused to serve him no matter his current pitiable situation. Sanderson had to order from Ed, her husband, who would serve whisky to a six-year-old. Ed seemed to like Sanderson better drunk than sober. Less of a threat? Earlier they'd been sitting at the bar and Hollis Edgerton from work had ambled in with his darts team and walked right up to Sanderson, swept his shot and beer back out of reach and said, "Hold up now, Sandy, yo, what the hell is this?" Walter had dragged Hollis down bar where their whispers carried: girlfriend left him, some other fucker, house burned down. Let the poor boy be. Hollis had apologized, hadn't heard, man, shit, bro, sorry to hear it, he'd tried to buy him a shot of Wild Turkey and for his trouble had gotten hammered by Cynthia who said for all the bar to hear that buying a drunk a drink is a fucked up way to be somebody's friend no matter what he'd been through. Sanderson smiled at her as she blasted Hollis, took note of her concern, translated it into desire. He saw himself behind her, her elbows splayed out across the bar, bangs in her eyes, her jean skirt hiked up over the metal drink cooler so shiny so cold to the touch. She must have read his thoughts, for the look she gave him told him to go home and forget all about it, fat chance, don't hold your breath, when hell freezes over, all these tired sayings one right after the other, on and on in one quick scornful look in his general direction.

Ed served Walter, and Walter bought two of everything, claiming that he was Noah about to climb aboard his ark. Sanderson made him punch up not once but twice the only song that worked for Sanderson anymore, Otis Redding's "I've Been Loving You Too Long (to Stop Now)," and he waited for that meteoric moment when Otis begs his darling,

I'm down on my knees please don't make me stop now. They drank the hours away in their dark corner. People in the light, friends of Sanderson's, nodded his way, offered sympathetic frowns, raised their bottles. After a couple of drinks, Walter went to the men's, and Sanderson got up and walked slowly to his car.

Alone in the night and the Ford was floating, taking the streets between the bar and her house so knowingly he hardly had to steer. As he took corners, his new life, which he'd managed to collect since the fire—clothes and cans of food, a tent, a Coleman stove—shifted about in the back-seat. He'd been living in his car. There were plenty of people willing to take him in, lend him a guest bed, considering his circumstances, but he preferred the martyrmobile, itself a gift from a car-flush uncle. He liked not having to talk to anyone in the a.m., liked the fact that in the Ford the bar was open twenty-four/seven.

"Bingo," Sanderson cried as he swung onto her street and spotted the beat-to-hell Toyota pickup in her drive. The bike sculpture was lit up from the porch light left on, no doubt, for her lover. Studying it, Sanderson felt himself become it: parts ancient and rusty, other parts shiny and new, past and present welded into something altogether different that did not work at all.

He inched the Ford into the drive, and as his bumper

nosed the trailer hitch of the pickup, he felt an odd lifting, strange and sudden and unsettling, and when he realized what it was—joy, pleasure, maybe even bliss—he shook with a silent, tearless crying. Drunk, cold, smelly, his woman left him for somebody else, his house burned to the ground, and what did he feel but oh so free and happy.

He knew he ought to stop right then and there. Toss an empty into the yard, maybe fuck the sculpture up somehow, let her know he was still alive and not well. Then bolt, head over to Umstead Park, set up his tent. Maybe there were some nurses camping out over there tonight. A threesome of nurses who would cook for Sanderson and wash his clothes in a creek and dry them on stones by the fire while the four of them warmed themselves in his new domed tent.

Problem was, he'd burned his house down and she had not come back. He had taken a drink, which was far worse a fate: a domicile wasn't so hard to come by as a liver. He missed his high school yearbooks and his Mott the Hoople albums, but this was all about sacrifice. He'd lit a fire to his old life, watched it rise above the rooftops and blow away, and there had not even been a single phone call from her. He kept looking for her to break through the crowd the night of the fire. He was wrapped in a purple blanket, some neighbor lady's, and he kept looking for her to break through and join him up under the neighbor-blanket. Soon after the breakup he had managed to get to her good friend Debbie with his side of the story, and the day after the fire he called up Debbie to give her the news. She'd heard already. I am so sorry, Sandy, what can I do? No mention of Her. Sanderson had to finally suck up and ask: had anyone told her?

"Oh, she's out of town," said Debbie. "Went somewhere with that guy."

"What guy?"

"That new guy she sees."

"What's his name?"

"She never said."

"What did she say, Debbie?"

Debbie clammed up, seemed embarrassed to have said anything at all, which left Sanderson to sneak some on his own. He staked out her house after work. It wasn't hard to go unnoticed in his uncle's big pitiful Ford Fairlane. He found a spot a few houses down where he could see but not be seen, and many a night he'd spent there, drinking and listening to talk radio or a baseball game, eating from cans and bags of chips, if at all. Her lover came for the first time three days after he began his surveillance. She was with him—they both climbed out of the pickup, he even went round to open the door for her, something Sanderson had never seen the point in himself, especially if you were driving a beat-to-shit death trap with muddy tires. They walked arm in arm to the door, kissed on the porch, lingered there underneath the light as if putting on a show for Sanderson. It was a sight, damn sure was. He could have lived another hundred years and not seen anything so grisly but he could not turn his head, no way.

So far he had merely observed. He mounted evidence, which he documented in a pocket-size spiral notebook he kept on the dashboard of the Ford along with all his other vital paperwork. When the time came for action, he would know it, and now it had come, tonight was the night. Here he was in the driveway, had the fucker blocked in. *No way out,* he wrote in his pocket spiral.

He reached beneath the seat for a fresh pint, broke the seal, and sat back in the sprung seat to sip himself up for the moment. He hadn't really planned anything to say, for he would forget it all anyway in the heat, and besides, what did it matter what he said to them? They knew why he was here, what he wanted. They probably knew that better than he did himself.

It got late and the pint got low, then empty. Sanderson cracked the seal on his backup, turned the radio on, and listened to a talk-show host berate his callers for their stupid opinions. Beside the Ford, cigarette butts heaped in a pile in the grass. There were no other cars out, only cats slinking and screeching, and once he spotted a possum waddling around the side of the house where she kept the trash cans, and he was glad to share the night with these stealthy creatures who did their business in the dark. He spoke to them warmly, and they offered their condolences, as if they knew just from looking at the angle of his repose in the front seat of the Ford how much misery he was shouldering.

He did not mean to nap, but even when the policeman woke him with the butt end of a flashlight tapping on his window, he did not think it a terrible idea, given the weight of what lay ahead.

He cracked the window an inch. The policeman was standing in a gray, sickly light, which took Sanderson a few seconds to realize was dawn. Mist rose from the lawn. He heard a paper slap pavement down the street.

"Step out of the vehicle, please," said the policeman.

Sanderson squinted to read the officer's name tag. His name was Britt and he was bulky and very black-skinned. He had no hair at all. Sanderson was glad he had ditched Walter, who would have had things to say about this officer Britt, none of them too respectful.

"Good morning, Officer Britt," said Sanderson.

"I asked you to step out of the car, sir."

Officer Britt leaned toward the crack in the window. Sanderson smelled coffee on his breath, which reminded him of his own breath, and the fact that he was quite possibly breaking more than one law this early in the morning. It didn't seem fair at all to have been waked from what was surely a dream of reconciliation into a world where you were guilty before you were even allowed to brush your teeth.

Sanderson climbed out of the car slowly. He wobbled a little and grabbed hold of the door to steady himself, and Officer Britt inquired as to how much he'd had to drink, and Sanderson said he couldn't really say, he'd just woken up, give him a minute to get his head clear.

"You got any weapons in the car?" said Officer Britt.

"Not unless you count a tent pole," said Sanderson.

"Put your hands up on the car, spread your legs."

Sanderson did as he was told. Officer Britt was light-fingered and even though it was crazy, Sanderson thought how good it felt to be touched by someone, even a black, a man, a cop.

"Okay," said Officer Britt when he had frisked Sanderson up and down. He asked Sanderson his name and checked his driver's license and his registration, which was in his uncle's name, his own car, Sanderson explained rather patiently to the officer, having been burned up in a recent fire, which claimed also his house and all his worldly possessions.

"Sorry to hear about that," said Officer Britt.

"Oh, I set fire to it myself."

"That won't too smart," said Officer Britt. He was checking over the registration, and Sanderson got the feeling he did not believe much that was coming out of Sanderson's mouth. This hurt a little.

"See, she left me. I wanted her to come home."

"Which home was it you were wanting her to come home to?"

"Say what?"

Officer Britt spoke slowly and bit his consonants, as if he thought Sanderson did not speak English.

"I asked how she's going to come home to you if you burned your durn house down?"

"I figured we could stay in a motel."

"This the same woman whose property you're trespassing on?"

Sanderson realized for the first time that she had called the cops on him. Couldn't she have come out to shoo him away? He wanted badly to be angrier than he was. What was wrong with him this morning? He felt like lying down in the grass, going limp like a protester on television. He felt like letting his bones dissolve into an act of aggressive nonviolence and letting Officer Britt call a backup to help lift him onto a stretcher, upon which he would be carried out into the country by four burly cops, pallbearer silent and reverent, to a place where his domed tent rested in a spot by a creek. Officer Britt appeared very serious, as if he was trying to remember something, the rights he was about to read to Sanderson perhaps. What rights would those be?

"She told you I'm trespassing?"

"That's what this is called, sir. She don't want you here, it's called trespassing. Why you want to block her in? She can't even get out her driveway."

"Oh, I'm not blocking her in. I mean, I know she's blocked in, too, but that's only because he's parked behind her. He's the one blocking her in. I'm blocking him in."

"I'm not going to get into any of that. What I'm going to do right now is ask you to follow me over to my vehicle. Can you walk okay?"

"Of course I can walk."

Officer Britt took Sanderson's arm anyway. He led him over to the cruiser and delivered him into the backseat and asked for the car keys, which Sanderson said were in the ignition. He'd worn the battery down listening to an all-night talk radio show. This he had done deliberately, so he could not move the car even if asked, but Officer Britt managed to get the car started anyway, and Sanderson felt like crying as he watched his uncle's car bounce into the street and come to a noisy rest by the curb in front of her house.

Officer Britt got out and went to the door. She answered his ring immediately, and as she asked him in he got a glimpse of her, dressed in one of his old T-shirts and a pair of pajama bottoms. He checked the windows to see if her lover was spying on him from another room but saw nothing at all but the earliest sun bouncing off the glass.

"I hate that sculpture," said Sanderson to Officer Britt when he climbed back in the car with his clipboard. "Don't you hate that sculpture right there?"

Officer Britt had donned a pair of glasses in order to complete his paperwork. He turned to look at Sanderson slumped in the backseat, then cut his eyes toward the work of art in question.

"She declined to press charges, Mr. Sanderson. But she's going down to the station little later on to get a restraining order sworn out on you. You know what that means, Mr. Sanderson?"

"It means she loves me?"

Sanderson thought he heard Officer Britt laugh, but maybe it was himself he heard, and maybe it was the sound of some other emotion. He went ahead and smiled anyway, as if he had said something funny and people admired him for his ability to laugh away life's unfairness.

"It means you are not to come within one hundred yards of her at any time. It means you are not to contact her, and you can't be passing out in her driveway, and you can't be acting like you acted last night."

How else am I going to act, Sanderson wanted to ask. Just tell me this: what else am I supposed to do with this love? Where am I supposed to put it, now that she's gone and found herself another lover? Sanderson managed to stop himself from saying such a pitiful thing, for he knew that to Officer Britt, to everyone else in the world, it was not love that made him act this way. He realized that to the rest of the world he was a sore loser, if not a plain old loser, and that to them, the only thing he was in love with was a misery of his own making.

But those people would not know real love if it came for them at daybreak, tapping a flashlight against their window, ordering them out of their vehicle, reading them their rights. Like the good officer Britt, who was asking Sanderson if he had someplace to go this morning.

But Sanderson, thinking he was bound to come too close to her and get himself busted, was thinking about his rights.

Aside from the right to deny his love, which he'd already blown, it seemed he had no rights. There exists no protection for those left behind—the law sides with the leavers—and the only order he was bound by was the love he held on to even now. She might make it official that he could only love her from a distance, but so long as he did not abandon his love, there were no boundaries. What he did in its service—burn his house down, take a drink, block her lover's pickup in her drive—was sanctioned by laws simpler and larger than the ones that had landed him in the back of this cruiser.

How could they use against him anything he said in the name of his love? Sanderson was halfway out with his story before he even knew what he was going to say, and it felt right to say it even to a cop.

"The last night she spent with me, I tricked her into coming over to my house. I called her up and told her I didn't trust myself not to drink and would she come over there and sit with me for a while. She'd already mailed me my key back and I didn't ask her for my key back, I didn't want it back, I wanted her to keep it forever. Anyway, she rang the damn doorbell. I was lying in the bed, in the dark, and I hated hearing that doorbell ringing, while I was lying there in the dark, waiting for the woman I loved to come home to me, knowing I'd driven her away."

Officer Britt put his clipboard on the dashboard of the cruiser, and Sanderson thought he heard him sigh, but it could have been the creak of his holster as he relaxed into the seat, it could have been, instead of a sigh, some sign that he wanted to hear what Sanderson had to say.

"She lay down next to me in bed and we were talking and I was telling her how I loved her and wanted her back and she was tired from work and after a while she fell asleep. I was just about as happy then, listening to her breathing in her sleep, as I'd ever been. I mean, I felt bad for how I got her to come over to the house, I wasn't really all that in danger of drinking, no more than I've been since she left me, but I also felt so right to have her there in bed beside me, even though she had on all her clothes and her car keys were lying on the edge of the bed. I got up and put a blanket over her and she was dead asleep and after a while I fell asleep myself."

"Mr. Sanderson," said Officer Britt. "We need to get you squared away."

"Sometime in the night, late, I woke up and I moved close to her and took her in my arms and she let me and we slept like that for a while, and then I started kissing her and at first she just froze, but then she started to kiss me back some and all of a sudden she sat right up in the bed and said, 'I am not going to feel bad about this tomorrow, I'm not,' and then she took off her clothes and we went at it."

"Mr. Sanderson, I don't care to hear the details of your love life with your former girlfriend. What I care to hear is where you want to go right now. I can't let you stay here, you know."

"I ain't bragging, I don't have anything to gain by lying to you. I already lost everything, can't bring it back with lies. I'm telling you the truth, sir, nothing but. I did not give a damn about satisfying myself and it was the best love I'd ever made. I just concentrated on making her feel good so she'd see how capable I was after all, and it worked. You can tell, you know. It's obvious when you're satisfying the woman you love and for us men there's no better feeling in this world. You know what I'm talking about, don't you, Officer?"

"I hear you," Officer Britt said reluctantly.

"I felt like everything was going to be fine then. She was making some serious noise, she wasn't trying to hide it, how good it felt to be with me again, and then all of a sudden her cries turned to sobbing and I was holding her face in my hands and I will tell you what, Officer, I could of lived a thousand years without figuring out that her face was wet with tears and not sweat worked up from pleasure."

Officer Britt was silent. He stared out the window at the sculpture, and for a minute it seemed he was about to answer Sanderson's question about whether he liked it, but then Sanderson started talking again and Officer Britt reached gently for the clipboard and put it on the seat next to him. He started the car, eased away from the curb. Sanderson, watching his uncle's car slide out of sight, turned around for a last look at the house, but all he could see was the sculpture, which struck him in the weak light as monstrous, something evil he'd had a hand in creating. Sanderson felt his blood sugar dropping, his body begging for more booze, but he knew another drink would not take care of the emptiness he felt, as he'd given away some sacred private part of them to a stranger, a fucking cop.

"What I'm going to suggest is you get somebody to pick that car up for you, okay?" said Officer Britt. "I don't want you coming back over here, even to pick up your car."

"Just take me home," said Sanderson when they were out of her neighborhood.

"I thought you said you burned your house down."

"You aren't going to arrest me for that?"

"Didn't kill nobody, did you?"

"No."

"Collect any insurance?"

Sanderson hadn't gotten around to filing. It didn't seem right, collecting money off a statement made by bottomless and eternal love. As Officer Britt drove him farther and farther away from her, Sanderson kept busy thinking about all the terrible things in this world that he would never, ever do.

Smoke from Chester Leading
Me Down to See Dogman

Upstairs I found smoke in the pockets of my daddy's striped shirts. Hovering in the mouths of his cowboy boots like steam coming off a cauldron. In my mama's top two drawers, smoke up under her fold-in-private things. Smoke in my nostrils, smoke curling round the coils of my ears.

Smoke from the broiling steak that way downstairs they were calling Chester drove me to raise my hand like I had a question and search the dark hall for the cord to the hideaway steps. Bare-bulb attic light turned boxes marked CHRISTMAS, HATTERAS, and BRIC-A-BRAC: MANTELPIECE a chicken-skin yellow. Chester smoke rose from them. I sat down on HATTERAS and hugged the stooped me that hid there for a half hour, bent up under the eave slope, straddling the attic ribs. Dogman, dogman calling to me for the first time in weeks.

I was careful not to breathe too hard lest insulation get

sucked up inside me. It happened before. Men came to insulate and I climbed up to watch them unroll the thick pink blankets like sleeping bags, me thinking, all right now, hide out from the craziness in the kitchen, camp out up under the eaves. A voice called me down out of the way and I obliged and this is when it happened, me standing at the foot of the ladder, my head flung back so far my mouth led straight to my belly. A stray tuft went right down me, disappeared inside.

Something like that, bring it back up, it cuts you twice, better just to live with it. It's possible to go on ahead, carrying such inconveniences; lots of people got holes in their hearts they don't even notice after a while. So after making noise about suing some company's ass off, which they shut him up by saying should I have been allowed to wag-tail down there like a table-scrap dog, my daddy made best-insulated-belly-in-the-world jokes at me for a month, the length of his memory even if you were to shoot him. And I didn't even miss any school days, it happening in high summer, but that pink tuft I carry within.

Up rose the voice my mama uses when company comes, blue, curvy, beautiful to a fault. I waited until she'd quit calling to make my descent. Frontwards down the hinged ladder, Chester smoke thickening. Don't plunge or you'll get the bends, I told myself while climbing down, and this self-administered advice tickled my insulated belly, allowing smiles for everyone when I entered the kitchen.

Where there was smoke from Chester mixed with Tareyton and pot smoke, where there was glass sparkle, plates chinking, King Crimson on the tape player. Some lady with Cleopatra bangs pasted to her forehead played the spoons, the men in the room watching her knit skirt surf a fishnetted knee. Daddy pulled a wide knife from the slotted block it took him six Saturdays to make, everybody bunched up to see Chester sliced. My mama and daddy continue to work their way through this world in the back of restaurants because they say it's the only type job where the laughter don't come in a can. Half of the restaurant help shows up at our house weekly to dispose of items they decide are overstock.

Greasy oven door banging down: Chester! George the sous-chef leaped toward the ceiling, jerked the beaded cord of the exhaust fan. As it cranked up, smoke shifted above our heads like flute-charmed cobras. Before I gave up Dogman I would have felt excitement in a situation similar, as if I was part of a group of older people just about to move off somewhere together. But that was before I gave up Dogman and at age fifteen and some change discovered what it is about groups of people.

—Cut the music down, called Daddy, grinding his knife in whetstone swirls I could tell he thought sexy.

—What exactly *is* Chester? A drunk woman asked this. I knew she was drunk because her words managed to sound lazy and exuberant at the same time.

—If you mean what cut, technically I believe Chester is a London broil. Somebody down in front said this without turning around, words passed overhead like bodies on stretchers.

Waving back the crowd with his hot mat mitt, Daddy pulled the oven rack out as far as it'd go, letting Chester bask and steam, laying him out for the group of them who'd named their dinner just to have an inside joke to get them through the deep drift of upcoming Tuesdays at work. Even Mama seemed moved as she stared at Chester who rose from the pan like a steep-sided island, greasy seas boiling at the bottom of his cliffs. Daddy, thumbing black plastic spatulas, shoveled Chester onto a cutting board and sliced so professional skinny you know he went to school for it. He's CIA, all the way up to Hyde Park, New York, to take his degree, though Mama, when she's pissed, calls his alma mater Culinary Institute of Alabama instead of America, says he don't know snail from doorstep slug.

Chester's carved sides curled into the bubbly sea. Everything went grainy then, everyone had Dick Tracy dotted faces, corduroyed foreheads. Dogman, Dogman, loud and clear. They started to line up with their plates to their breasts like grade school or prison and before the first slice slapped plate I was out the door and half down the hill, smoke from Chester pushing and pulling me.

MY COUSIN MILLY'S the one took me up there first. Dogman's always been so-so to her, take or leave, like cigs snuck in the bathroom during assembly. Though I have learned that people all the time take you to see things they don't themselves appreciate nor understand. Museums for one. They'll bus you over, snake you single file behind a teacher who's looking only a water fountain that works. What do you owe those who bring you to places that touch or change you? Don't owe them jack. They're only vehicles, saggy camels delivering you to the sphinx. Ride them until they're tongue-waggy, rub and chafe until their humps are threadbare as back-porch throw rugs, tweak their ears when you want down and when you dismount, don't you *even* look back.

Milly knows this herself. Boys kept bringing her up to where Dogman's supposed to roam, hoping she'd what? Fall willing under the spell of their clunky desires got up in man-dog costume and sent to prowl the ridges? Dogman the local Loch Ness monster, rivaled around here only by the Baby Bridge and the irrigation pond they raked for Floyd Japarks's bloated corpse. Dogman standing in for the moonlit lane, the two Miller Lites, the skinny-dip, anything designed to introduce the friction. Dogman-as-aphrodisiac? It's like thinking old Darwin's seductive, which in a way his stuff sort of is, not that these boys would know Darwin's stuff if it chased them down and bit them.

Driving up to see Dog that first time, Milly leans into her big idea boy, away from the door and the sidewalks just beyond, like the car's hugging a constant curve. She wants to ask where he's taking her but don't. She's heard talk of Dogman and wants to be a witness but yet you can't come out and ask, you got to come up on him.

Dogman'll run from you as he lives and breathes.

Milly wants to say she's seen him, but the boys taking her up there don't have foremost in their minds the tracking down of Dogman. You have to know where to park and all. You got to learn to follow clotheslines through the head-high dark as if they were flashlight beams frozen for you. There's a sixth-sense semaphore out there, a complicated taking into account of things: crosstown sirens bouncing like hailstones off the sides of barns and train whistles shaking trees. One short and two long caterpillars underfoot. Smell the crunched grass not yet sprung back up. It's a question of putting yourself out there by turning yourself inside out, which most would not want to do even if they knew how.

One night Milly claims to see something. They're rounding the switchback on one of those logging roads that fork off Japarks Drive and come up on something standing there in the muddy crook. Moonlight strikes the puddle he straddles. Milly's fuzzed on details because she says the light loses out to the clouds as they watch, but when I doubt her to her face she comes up with something: drawn-up paw, cheek dribble, dangling tongue, drool-coated fang agleam. She describes *at* it, conjuring things I would have said myself if you asked me back then what he looked like.

She's back up there lots with that same boy, but when they go for a good month or two without a sighting she exchanges him for a few more. Sometimes she claims to see Dog for a second or two but always when he's running away or behind a tree. Like I said, it's to Milly like shoplifting Sucrets or sneaking into the drive-in. She doesn't *need* it. Soon as she gets her license, Uncle Houston gives her that castoff Astro to drive, Mill loads the front seat with her big-haired girlfriends and goes looking Dog like four nights a week. Suddenly above using love to get up that hill. Love changes shape when you pass your driving test and get given a car, even an Astro the greenish of bad teeth. For some, this is independence: a half ton of sprung seat and dangly rearview, life course sighted by a hood ornament. I might could feel this way myself had not Milly told me about Dogman, had I not been born knowing what's a vehicle and what teaches you things.

But maybe I was born not knowing squat, just like the rest of the world. Maybe I was nothing special until that moment I stood gawking up at black-attic heaven and received from on high a piece of glass disguised as county fair cotton candy. Had I stood a little to the left or shut my trap I would have grown up to be like my parents or Milly. Instead I carry within O pink hurt everlasting. I breathe, I bleed: invisible harm done with every doggy-dog pant.

Overstock rum from the restaurant flooded a weekend way back when. Seems like forever ago, but it was after Milly got her license, which she's only had them six months so it must have been spring. Milly came by the house that Saturday. Overstock oysters roasted in foot tubs; there must have been twenty people from the restaurant, which led me to wonder was it even open or had they called an overstock strike. Me and Milly sneaking sweet rum punch and eavesdropping: heard one man say about his wife smack in front of her that all she ever did in this world was sit around and wait for books to come out in paperback, which Milly thought was funny but which got away with me so bad I begged Milly to go to ride.

Which she agreed to only if I'd hunker down when she got whistled at, which I agreed to.

Wasn't much whistling, wasn't much hunkering. Mill took back roads through that neighborhood called Stairstep, where houses hang half off the ridge like they've been left there by high water. I could have got offended—Mill not wanting to be seen with me—but the main thing was we get up there and find Dogman.

We wound up Japarks, too fast past the unfinished church, skimpy tithing having left the roof a patchwork of shingle and tin. I used to ride up there on my bike when I was little and the church was an ancient ruin to me then, back in my junior archeologist period when all I wanted to do was dig up buried cities, cannonballs, dinosaur bones. What cured me finally was a program on public tube which told how these archeologists dig for years sometimes and don't uncover much but a broken vase. Vase the narrator pronounced in the snooty-ass British manner—vozz—which, hell, I guess I would call it that too if it took me a year to dig one up.

—I wonder what do they call that style of architecture, said Milly, inclining her whole body toward the church.

—Run out of money, I said.

—That particular style you just mentioned could describe this entire town.

Milly's all-of-a-sudden prissy diction made me picture her

marrying a recruit in a few years time just to escape from our town. One day on base she'd blink awake on her dribbly pillow to stare at pink scalp beneath crew-cut stubble, hair running in feathery arrows like bones of filleted flounder and Milly hating fish. But I could not stop and feel sorry for her. Not when we were on our way up to see Dogman.

—Slow damn down some.

She sped up until we passed a car she thought she knew. She whistled, I hunkered. From the floorboard I watched Mill's foot hesitate in a float between brake and gas before she decided she couldn't be seen with me and heeled the gas. I came out of my crouch. It's all vanity. On a personal quest, what do you care if someone spots you with your weird little cousin? Vanity or vengeance one, I decided, thinking of Mama and Daddy and how they thought they were getting over with their overstock parties, how many ways they'd found to make those binges sound rightfully theirs: food going to waste, low wage and long hour, customers getting gouged. That last one I loved best, them taking pity on the poor customers not while at work but at home and only when there's a makeshift holding tank, Daddy's beat blue pier-fishing cooler, full of lobsters for them to tong at and name crazy names. In my head I started writing a song called "People Got Their Wrong Wrong Reasons," which Milly interrupted the very first stanza of.

—We ain't going to see him tonight.

—And why aren't we?

—Too damn dark, she said, tossing her tongues-of-flame-licking-headrest hair.

But we did see him, or I did, no thanks to Milly, who did everything she could to drive him away. I had to reach over and crank the car off so we could coast up the logging trail at the end of Japarks. The Astro rocked to a stop in a little lake swallowing the trail. To reach land we had to do splits. Milly kept up a bitchy stream I wagered my parents could hear over the Apache war cry album they loved to throw on around this time of the evening. It was *bad* dark out, limbs-clawing-you-before-you-even-know-you're-up-on-them dark, Milly shadowing me after those first wet steps through the backhoe-tread puddles. Plainly she was a vehicle; the camel had kneeled.

I pushed on through the dark, Milly siamesing me all the while, which cut down some on what I could pick up from that side. I was thinking all sorts of things like who do we owe, for what, how much, and why was it that I out of everybody—Milly and her horny boys, Mama and Daddy and their vengeful coworkers—got chosen to see good in the dark.

We came around a bend where the lights of the town glowed beneath and there he stood, so close that I could see the pipe cleaners curling out of his suit-coat breast pocket, white padded wires bent into tiny walking sticks. I could see

the rusted buttons of his overalls and hear the hooks rub-
bing against them when his chest heaved with shallow pants,
the whiskered face skin which in that little light was the up-
underside gray of washed-ashore fish. I could see his hand
draw into the curl of a run-over paw.

Seeing him made me want to gargle up some great strange
yell. Quick, something inside me said, hook me up to a hot
machine, one what sucks up the blood unleashed from that
swallowed piece of pink. I turned to Milly to see did she hear,
for I couldn't tell if I'd cried out or dreamed such a cry, but
Milly was not there. I clutched my chest, for I could feel it
inside, hot salty river running wild.

THAT WAS THE END of me going to see Dogman
with Milly. For a while that was the end of me going up there
at all, but knowing that he was out there, that every night half
the town was out stalking him, making up all kinds of hokey
lore about him—that he was hybrid offspring of a Fice and
a woman from down around Garland, that he was escaped
mental, that he was a hermaphrodite and did his dog routine
to cover up nature's cruel error, that he bit Reggie Boyette to
the bone, that he was Sue Talkington's uncle—drew me back
up the mountain.

I could find him every time. I could leave the house do-

ing everything it's possible might not allow me to locate
him—wear flip-flops and gym shorts and that's all in an ice
storm, take the loop over Beaucatcher Mountain which it's
five miles around that way, crash through the bush like a
backhoe—here he would still be waiting on me. No, I did
not ever try to talk to Dog. No, I did not try to feed him
tainted burgers from the Sonic or inquire as to his day job.
All that concerned me in those days was that I could walk
straight up to him.

Which I could do always, which nobody else could do, and
which, this got around. Big-haired girlfriends of Milly's came
rumbling by the house, their boyfriends' low Camaros idling
like off-cycle washing machines out by the curb. Milly all of
a sudden did not mind me sitting prominent in the sprung
seat of her Astro, out the window went the system of hunker
when whistled at. *Vanity.* She never said word one to me about
what she'd seen up there that night; turned out she needn't,
since I heard it all from everybody else and it was all wrong,
wronger even than the reasons that caused her to repeat it. At
the overstock parties the restaurant people would draw me
aside to ask how did I do it, where was Dogman that minute,
let's get up a posse and head up there now. *Vengeance!* Beat
down people seeking someone to beat further down, and that
the sad history of this world and my own mama and daddy a

part of it, furious at me for not fingering a crude map in the bowl of overstock chocolate mousse held out to me one night, which they planned to carry up the ridge and illuminate with Tiki torches so that later, in the short-tempered steam of their kitchen shifts they could have that creepy hour to bring up and brag about. Wrong-reasoned people of this earth tugging and gnawing at me! How could I watch them turn Dog into the kind of anecdote trumped up to while away the tick of a time clock? What could I do but give up Dogman entirely?

This I did to become those three most invisible and untalked-to things on earth: a younger cousin, a quiet kid with braces and scruples, the teenaged son of your host at a party where tables are crammed with pricey things to slurp and chew.

Then Chester. Smoke from Chester. But how come Chester and not the fifty pounds of mahimahi liberated two weeks previous and broiled in shifts that kept the house smelled up fishy for a week? Why Chester? Who Chester? I had managed to stay away for six months during which not once had Dogman been spotted. Milly had given up searching. She'd started going out with a boy home from boot camp, my prophecy come true, though I did not relish being right. Obviously she'd outgrown Dogman, did not speak of him, didn't speak to me at all. For a while people would bug me about it, but after a few weeks of my shruggy smiling back they left off.

Then smoke sending me upstairs, away from daddy demonstrating butterfly techniques on a piece of Chester did not fit into the pan. Smoke sending me up to where those pink blankets stretched into the dark angled eaves like the curve of this earth, where I hunkered, wondering, Why Chester? Who Dogman?

Scene of the crime. Often I retreated here, despite its dangers—sentimental bric-a-brac from some earlier innocent time neatly boxed and shoved into corners, utter and airless isolation of the stripe not healthy for a soul likes to go around feeling like he's a universe of only, and of course the acres of pinkness beckoning. Lay me down to sleep. I thought I could escape there, but smoke rises and Chester smoke, hell: it's only purpose was to hunt me down, root me out, send me off on my final journey. Why Chester? No real reason except for my random time done come. Oh I could claim it was the name Chester triggered something deep and significant within, I could up and decide the senseless slaughter of some cow they named a sliver of was what got away with me that day. The truth was, as usual, way less sexy: number come up.

As for Dog, well: Dogman was Dogman. Every town had one: the man who crows like a rooster at first light, the woman who pushes a grocery cart crammed with cats whose flea-ridden house has to be fumigated by neighborhood decree.

They're everywhere. They ain't right. Heard recently of a woman down in Garland who shows up in Family Foods wearing on her head a pair of sheer panties across which is Magic Markered the word *Head*. Dogman's just another one of these. Not right in the head. Man thinks he's a dog.

By the time I got through settling big questions, Chester smoke had driven me down out of the attic. Back in the kitchen, two crooked fingers of smoke settled in front of my nostrils. I slipped out the side door while everyone was loading their plate with bloody slabs and in no time was up the hill past the church ruined or unfinished one, didn't matter, immaterial, couldn't tell, so socked in by Chester smoke.

There's big moon up there that night, all the yard art of upper Stairstep lit by it, scum water glowing green in birdbaths, satellite dishes tilting their wide mouths to the heavens. I'd never been up there when there was this much moon, never seen Dogman on a night so bright. I tried to abandon myself to that sixth-sense semaphore but nothing came, everything was blocked, Chester smoke canceling out everything. There was a rustling below, voices rising above a throaty chorus of cars. Next hairpin I looked down to see a line of folks coming up the trail, each of them carrying a candle in a bag of sand. Overstocked from the restaurant of course. I heard my mama's blue curvy words, my father's whiskyed ones, all of them climbing to the rhythm of spoon against fishnet knee. Crouching on the shoulder of a switchback, I spotted Milly sliding out of the car with her boyfriend in tow. In that praise be quiet that comes whenever the Astro is cranked off, Milly turns to him and says, We'll see him, we're going to see him this time, my little cousin can find him every time.

Would he show for such a little cousin like me? My senses were dulled by Chester smoke, the burnt smell of him, the carboned taste of him which I didn't take bite one but still this purloined meat had somehow ended up rank within. Chester, too, in the bellies of those fools following me. *Dogman come on and show yourself so I can turn you over to them and go damn home.*

But he didn't. Chester smoke thickened the higher we climbed; it rose off the hillside until the whole forest was on fire with it, and I ran from it and into it too. Seeing me run, they followed: vengeful workers, big-haired girls, Mama, Daddy, Milly, and her skinhead ticket out of here. Half the town was behind me when I tripped and fell to the ground.

That pinkness within: something too dangerous to let back out, better to let it settle. But what with all the running it had begun to bloat up big as Chester, and besides, what had my suffering brought me but the ability to see good in the dark?

Up there on the ridge, moon hitting me like spotlights, I

mashed my fingers to my face like a baby'll do you. I found my lips and parted them. Fingernails tapped teeth, grazed stalactite tonsil. What the rest of them found when they came around the bend was a boy making noises known neither to dog nor man, trying to bring up that piece of pink but in the process flushing Dogman out from a cloud of Chester smoke.

Couple Strike It Rich
on Second Honeymoon

A COUPLE, WRETCHED IN LOVE, in a car, on an interstate. On a muggy Saturday morning in October they left behind the city where they lived and headed west. Their history was more ragged than most: they had been together for two manic years, bruised themselves silly during an endless third, were apart for a year, and finally, because they could not let go of each other, were together again in a car, on an interstate, headed toward a loosely planned weekend of reconciliation.

This city, which held their entire history, was in the middle of a state offering both mountains and coast. There was debate about which would be the best backdrop for their reconciliation. Kevin said it was up to Ann, but he knew that being a nonnative of the state, Ann would let him choose in the end, and she did. Once, years ago, Kevin had agreed to spend the weekend with a girl whose father owned a condo on the side of a ski slope; on the way up the mountain she had broken up with him, and because he wanted badly to have a free place to stay while he slid unskillfully down a blanket of man-made snow, he had allowed himself to finish out the weekend, sleeping on the couch, listening to his ex whisper late at night to some unspecified party on a telephone whose cord reached just barely beyond the closed door of the condo's lone bedroom. It was the kind of scenario one admitted to only when half drunk, and it never made the kind of "can you believe I did that" story he hoped it would. Kevin had long regretted the stupidity of his choice, and it seemed to him if he chose now the same range of ancient mountains, his greedy miscalculation might be wiped clean from history.

Since Ann had announced her intention to give them another try, Kevin had thought a lot about history, and he was reminded of it by everything she said or did, like the way she was rifling unsatisfactorily through his tape box for something that, according to her, they had not heard four hundred times. To alleviate the weight of before, Kevin reminded himself that Ann was not the woman he had fallen in love with and that this was a grand thing, a redemptive glorious fact that would save them this time around. He looked at her hair streaming out of the window and congratulated himself on learning to love not who she was when he first met her but the woman she had become to him as he navigated all sorts of treacherous currents in his own psyche, and he had told anyone who would listen to him that this was what real love was, a frequent and vigilant gauging of your own reality, constant calibrations to include your lover in the world that would surely overwhelm you if you let it remain yours alone.

At thirty-two, he was a little old for such a realization, but he waited tables for a living.

"Think you'll ever tell me to get a real job?" Kevin said.

Ann looked up from the tape box, ahead toward the first soft smudge of the Blue Ridge instead of at him.

"Not unless we were to get a washer–dryer."

Because of his tips, Kevin could always be counted on for quarters, vats of them greasy with the oil of someone else's fingers. He did not like to touch them. While Ann was gone he had found a machine at the supermarket that would convert them to grocery money and he had devised ways to get them from pocket to bowl to plastic bag to machine without soiling his hands, but he knew, now that Ann was back, that she would insist on keeping them loose for the Laundromat. Surely there were other more important things to consider about her return. Like, for instance, the coupling that awaited them after they passed the daylight away and found a motel and ate a quick dinner and returned to their room for the hours of reconsummation he'd dreamed of nightly for the past twelve months.

"Sometimes I feel like what happened to us could have been so easily avoided," said Kevin.

He could tell from the way Ann watched a busload of schoolkids pass by in the next lane that she was not happy with this line of thought. He had tried not to bring up their rupture, but it did not seem possible that they avoid their past entirely, especially this weekend during which every word, every touch, had the potential to take them backward instead of forward. In her silence he began to sulk, terrified that she would tell him to turn back, forget about it, trip's off.

"Ninety percent of what happens to people could be easily avoided," she said.

So why even say such a thing, is this what she meant? What difference did it make now that they could have avoided their fate? Instead of avoiding it, they fell helplessly and headlong into it, and it was as messy and tortured as these things get, filled with accusations of betrayal and third parties and countless phone calls ending in hang-ups and doorbells rung at 3 a.m. There were witnesses called to corroborate alibis, letters steamed open, journals read, and underneath all this was an energy that reminded the both of them of the crazed spontaneity that characterized their first weeks together. In fact, it felt so much like their particular manner of falling in love that they both found ways to prolong it, needling and

provoking long after that point when other couples might
have shut down, given up.

"I guess you're right," Kevin said, though he wasn't at all
sure that he agreed. Some people, maybe most, were more
practical, measured, when it came to love. He had observed
in his friends' affairs an almost clinical tidiness, which he
found far more repulsive and destructive than their own fi-
ery breakup. Ann would probably pronounce him naive if he
made this point to her—she was fond of claiming that he
found what he was looking for, and never went looking without a quarry firmly in mind. He kept his mouth shut, tried to
think of ways to change the subject, but instead he changed
lanes, speeding up and drifting over to the left lane after the
bus was visible in his rearview mirror.

"I liked watching those kids," Ann said. "Anything's better
than the signs advertising all these hokey tourist traps."

Kevin preferred the billboards for Tweetsie Railroad and
Land of Oz theme parks to the leering kids, whose attention made him feel awkward and ancient, but because he was
being accommodating he accelerated until they were once
again alongside the bus, which seemed to be filled with a
football team and cheerleaders headed to a game. He tried
not to look, but when Ann said, Those girls think you're hot,
Kevin glanced past her to see a couple of bored cheerleaders

sharing a laugh over something he was sure he did not care to know.

Kevin was desperate for a segue to take him out of this silence and thought of saying, "And you? Do you think I'm hot?" But he was scared she'd say something ambivalent like, "I'm here, aren't I?" and he would have to agree with her being there beside him in the car, a fact so surprising to him still that he was not sure he wanted to examine it. There was another reason why the question was dangerous: she had had a lover for eleven months of the year they were apart. Only three weeks earlier she had gotten rid of him, and though he knew he should have waited to be with her until she was over her lover—she had waited only a week before taking up with this man after she left him—he felt that waiting (even if he could have managed it) would in this case be putting her lover's feelings before his own, and he wanted badly for her lover to stay up all night for weeks with a tumbler of iceless bourbon and a rekindled cigarette habit, listening as he had to scratchy record albums over which he had grieved the loss of girls back in high school.

As they began the climb into the Appalachians, Kevin plugged cassettes into the tape player and sang along brightly with songs they had shared while together. But he worried: about how to kill the daylit hours, for it was too early yet to find a motel and check in and he certainly did not want to appear too eager for that part of the two of them he had missed the most.

Kevin knew the area moderately well and several options occurred to him—a couple of antiques stores, a stretch of a river clogged so tightly with huge boulders that you could rock-hop a half mile either way. But he dismissed these ideas quickly, as he would never be able to focus on antiques and was sure his boredom would show, and as for the river, how could he expect to keep his hands off Ann in such awesome seclusion? They used to camp when they were together and what they liked most about nature was the erotic opportunities it provided. No, he needed something genuinely and newly distracting, something he would never have done when they were first together to keep at bay his eagerness and his anxiety.

Not three miles past the point where the highway crossed the Eastern Continental Divide, in the first of several tacky hamlets vying for tourists, Kevin found his solution. Along a two-mile stretch of otherwise scenic highway, a half-dozen gem mines competed for the leaf-season traffic. He seemed to remember his parents taking him and his sister to one of these places when they were in grade school, though the particulars were long lost to him. He knew that Ann would object because she did not care to throw darts at balloons when they visited carnivals, or enter sweepstakes or buy lottery tickets or any other of the ways in which he squandered money taking chances. Ann took chances of a more dangerous sort, and he had it in mind that aside from killing time he might also attempt some unspoken but obvious moral instruction about the types of chances one could take with impunity. He would be careful not to use this word for he was overly fond of it and had overused it in the past nine months and Ann had let him know more than once that impunity to her was a less than noble goal, if even an attainable one. We all get hurt and punish ourselves and find ways to punish those we care for the most, she'd said to him once. Though Kevin acknowledged the obvious truth in this statement, he nonetheless questioned her need to allow for such obligatory crime and punishment. This was back when he used to argue with her, before he found ways to love the person she had become.

Kevin swung suddenly into the dusty gravel lot of a gem mine. He chose one with a fruit stand attached to one end, so that Ann might assume he had stopped for apples, which were gloriously in season.

"Do they have cider?" she asked, and he said he was sure they did and he would buy some after they were through.

"Through what?"

"We're going gem mining."

She asked if he was kidding but without conviction, as if he expected such a response.

"Dead serious," said Kevin, and Ann resigned herself to it with a sigh, easing out of the shoulder harness so willingly that it occurred to him that she, too, might be going out of her way to keep things light and easy between them. Perhaps she had learned what he had learned in their time apart. For some reason this idea made him tremble, and he hesitated with the car door swung open until Ann said his name and nodded at the door and he saw that he was blocking a space for a van trying to pull in next to him.

"Counting your money?" said a heavy red-faced man climbing out of the passenger's side of the van. Before Kevin could answer, the man said, "You best take more than you planning on. I'll tell you, they'll lighten your wallet in these places."

The man's companion had hauled herself out of the driver's side and was alongside saying, "Don't listen to him, he'll spend all day out here, going broke for a four-dollar ruby."

"Is that how this works?" Ann asked when the couple was out of earshot. "You spend forty bucks on a four-dollar stone?"

That's the way everything works, Kevin thought. Quickly he hooked his arm in Ann's and drew her close as they scuffed through the gravel. "The Hope diamond was discovered here," he said.

"You don't say?"

"And the crown jewels of England."

"And the Rosetta stone?"

"And Liberace. He came shining up out of the muck. Some preacher unearthed him. Hosed him off and taught him to play piano and made a killing off him."

He felt so good going into the mine that he ordered the largest bucket available, which was the size of a washtub and took two high school boys to carry. They followed the boys through the office out under the shed covering the long, bench-lined sluice. The water running over the shallow chute appeared clear and cold. Kevin looked forward to placing his hands in its iciness. It was not until the high school boys had set their bucket down and found him a trowel and filled two trays to brimming with lumpy dirt that he remembered Ann, who seemed to be enjoying the sight of him enjoying himself. She looked amused and skeptical behind her sunglasses, which weren't necessary under the shadowed shed, and he wanted badly to kiss her and lead her right out of the shed into the rhododendron-clogged forest that rose steep-banked right alongside the gem mine. He imagined his fellow miners smiling as he and Ann gave themselves over to a passion that even children and crones would recognize as pure and deserving. He imagined applause as they returned to take their chances with trays of dirt.

They watched their neighbors sift the trays in the rushing water, washing away the dirt and picking through the rocks remaining at the bottom of the tray. When they felt confident they knew what they were doing they lowered their own trays in the water.

"We'll never get through this tub of dirt," Ann said.

"Might take us a week, but it will be worth it if we find what we're looking for."

"And what are we looking for?"

"Priceless jewels. Buried treasure. The mother lode."

"Right. So let's say there is something here, and we found it. How do you think our lives would change?"

Kevin shut his eyes tightly, as if doing so would make her take her question back. She got this way sometimes, querulous and analytical. Often Kevin worried that Ann was smarter than he was or, if not more intelligent, then more focused, less prone to distraction, delusion.

"Do you mean what would we buy with the money we got from selling our booty?"

Ann laughed. "No, that's not what I mean and you know it. We'd spend the money."

"No, we'd put it away for our children's college education."

Ann studied her tray. Kevin felt his stomach tighten, as it always did when she failed to acknowledge some reference to their future.

"Why don't we concentrate on unearthing our treasure first," he said. "Plenty of time to consider what it might do to us."

But she was hard at work already, shaking her tray lightly, watching the water wash away the dirt. She had a rhythm going that he envied, for he was too aware himself of what was at stake here, too conscious of the fact that they weren't really going to find anything but a few small bright stones they could buy, bagged, in the gift shop for far less than they'd paid for this bucket it seemed would take them a lifetime to work through.

And what if there was nothing there at all? Kevin reminded himself of the purpose of this venture: to kill some time until sundown, when he would have her back in the way that he'd dreamed about for months. He lost himself in thoughts of the two of them rolling across a king-size vacation bed, finding things to do to each other that were at once familiar and brand-new. He wanted so much from this night; he wanted it to be the first time they'd touched, and he wanted their touch to convince Ann of what they had and had almost lost.

He wanted her to regret leaving him, regret taking up with her lover, but he wanted these regrets to be tempered with impunity, for he would find the strength to forgive her for all her sins against him if she'd only stay put and trust her imagination this time.

Down the line the large man they'd spoken to in the parking lot bellowed so ridiculously that both of them dropped their pans in the water.

"Your friend seems to have hit the mother lode," Ann said.

The man was holding up a stone as big as a pecan. Kids had left their places on the bench to run down and gawk over his shoulder. It was a dull purplish—an amethyst, it looked like, crude but huge. The man's wife looked unimpressed, and later, when they passed by on the way out, she winked at Kevin and Ann and nodded at her husband, who was too thrilled by his find to speak.

"Gets what he pays for and it tickles him to death." The woman lingered long enough to say that she and her husband had renewed their vows the night before in a ceremony and were retracing their romantic getaway of thirty years earlier. Her husband called to her to come on, they were going to get their picture taken with their find, and Kevin imagined buying a newspaper and coming across this couple grinning blindly into the flash, a cheesy headline highlighting their renewed vows.

"That's great," Kevin said, after the woman had told them to have a blessed day and trundled off after her husband. "Isn't that great? I think I'll buy this place. We'll move up here and make people happy."

"What about the ones who come up empty?"

"They can buy another bucket. You can run the office and I'll stay out back, planting the jewels in the dirt."

"Great. I'll have to deal with the unhappy ones who want their money back."

"People know what the deal is. They know it and they want it anyway. It's a risk, sure, but isn't everything? You have to decide whether it's worth it or not, and sometimes you don't even have to decide. You just trust that it is."

Ann dropped her tray in the sluice. She stood up.

"What?" he said to her, but she was pushing the hair out of her eyes and looking away from him, and it seemed to Kevin like a year passed before she turned to him.

"I'll be in the car."

"Come on, Annie," he said. "All I'm saying is that there are worse ways to make fools of people."

"Give me the keys," she said.

Kevin handed them over. What else could he do? He knew

there would be no talking to her until she had cooled off, that these arguments were not won or lost but merely forgotten. He knew a thing or two about time and forgetting and forgiving and waiting with an expectation that kept you engaged with every breath, almost like, by dreaming hard of what you wanted, you were walking through the world you expected to find.

Kevin refilled his tray with more dirt and set to work washing mud from rocks of the sort he might have picked up in the parking lot, the kind crunching under Ann's shoes as she made her way to the car. But as soon as his tray was empty he felt an emptiness himself, which lingered even when the tray was brimming again. He kept at it anyway, for even though he knew he should be getting impatient and even irritated by his lack of success, he realized he'd paid far too much for this tub of muddy gravel, and it seemed to him irresponsible to leave even the slightest chance of a payoff for someone else to find.

The Golden Era of Heartbreak

AFTER SHE LEFT, the town where we lived grew flat as an envelope. Sound carried: the song of a truck driver showering five miles east. Nothing could block his dirge. Long-distance misery leaking across the flats while he scrubbed away the road grime. He, too, had come home to a top drawer cleared of underwear. I could hear him night and day, asking her forgiveness, beg your pardon, baby, for the times that she'd arrived home to find him gone. I knew from the rising strings that she'd never come back, that he would never get clean. Those strings: sweet Nelson Riddle arrangements, country meringue from the fifties. Pinnacle of lovelorn lament. Fine time for misery.

My house filled to the eaves with this song. Moths waved in the soaring orchestration. They dusted lampshades with it, painted the medicine-cabinet mirror. Up half the night trying not to listen, I reverted to an opinion I had given up forty years earlier, along about kindergarten: globes were wobbly lies. The earth was flat as the muted-by-miles-of-not-much-of-nothing notes of the trucker's song. Nowhere to hide and no escape, just sleep for the lucky and, for me, punishing runs.

After she left, I ran hundreds of miles along those low-shouldered roads. It got to where Mexican migrants would stop work to bring me a cucumber when I slashed past in the lethal early-afternoon heat. Then the hospital, where they gave me medicine that turned me into a loaf of bread. The cheerful foreign doc asked me what year it was and I told him pointedly—I mean to say that I got up in his face so close that his pocked scars from a wicked case of acne were craters on a magnified moon—that the major daily of our nation's capital was contaminated because she had scoured its ads in want, want, want—I always got stuck on that word—I said to the doc, Her want spreads spores like anthrax. Say anthrax in one of those places. Is it an irony that registers on anyone but the inmate that you're in there for behavior interpreted as less than rational, but when you say something crazy—which in that situation seems to me the norm—they shoot you full of more bread loaf? Though I confess I ate the ruffled paper cup that held my pills. I confess I'd have done anything to keep from returning to an earth leveled by her leaving.

SHE'D BEEN GONE for a year and a half and I had not heard word one. I knew where she had alighted and with whom, but had no street address, no lover's last name. Just major metropolitan area with this Rick she met at a conference. Work-related: how I hate having first scoured the want ads that brought us here to this town.

"You could just as easily hate the conference where she met him," said my sister when I complained about having helped Beth find the job. That was when I was still fool enough to commiserate with family members and worlds-at-large. Back before, one by one, they all turned on me. Went from suggesting acupuncture to signing me up for some extended-stay hospital. People have no sympathy for the brokenhearted because it's what they fear the most. They pretend it's as minor and obligatory as having your wisdom teeth pulled, getting your heart ripped from your chest, having feral mutts tug-a-war the bloody organ in your kitchen while you lean white-veined against the rusty refrigerator, drowning in schmaltzy string arrangements.

So I had no one—only the Mexican migrants who offered cucumbers and water from the boss man's cooler and must have recognized in my desperate stride a fellow alien. The only person I got around to trading words with was the laconic, chain-smoking Deb—or so her name tag read—who worked at the market where I purchased my few provisions. It was a sticky-floored, dirty-ceilinged store that Beth had favored over the chain grocery because after the dogwoods bloomed Deb and her coworkers would take out the magazines in aisle 7 and stock it with chilis and tortillas and even Spanish videos for the migrants.

One night I drove over to pick up my stock groceries: Band-Aids, ginger ale, saltines, bulk raisins, chicken broth, and white rice. I could live off this list for weeks at a time. And had been doing so, and the pounds sweated away in the eighteen-mile runs, and there weren't that many to leave puddling the road in the first place and so many times in the days after she left I would not have been able to tell you the correct use for, never even mind the name of, a fork.

"Give me one of those Pick Ten tickets," I said when I had my groceries all lined up on the belt. Deb wasn't there that night. In her place was a high school boy. His head was chubby and dripping with red-blond bangs. Used to be in a town like this you got beat up for wearing your hair long. Now the ones doing the beating are the only ones with their ears covered.

"You don't want one of them," said the boy.

So maybe he said *want* when he meant *need*—a mistake so many make. I had never been expert at figuring out what

I needed until Beth left. Then I knew: I needed her. I needed her groaning first thing in the morning when I set the alarm to the local gospel station and our day began with a Mass choir filling even the shoe-strewn closet bottoms with sonic interpretations of the word *Jesus*. Her tireless interest in the narrative of how we happened to find each other—that miracle recounted, with much attention paid to the extraordinary odds of it happening in this maddeningly flat world—how could I not need that? Each time she asked for it, I felt as if I were narrating Genesis. How humans came sweet and innocent up from the earth. I believed I breathed and ate and performed reasonably well at one activity or the other before we met, but in telling that story over and again, in having it received with such lusty anticipation, I came to believe that my life started the moment I met her, the moment we laid waste to those insurmountable odds.

Odds are terrifying if you let yourself obsess over them. In the case of the Pick Ten lottery, I was not interested in the odds. It was a spontaneous thing, asking the cashier for a ticket. I had never once wasted money on such. But I did not care for being refused. I especially disliked being rejected by this boy whose sullen mannerisms implied that the wonder I had known with Beth was nothing more than some sappy song he'd scowl at while scanning radio stations. I believe I did nothing more than push his doughy chest with my fingers. I remember still the squishiness I encountered where I was expecting breastbone. Surely I was as shocked as he was.

"Hole up," he said. Then: "Dude, what the hell?"

I held out a bill—a twenty, for which he made loud change. He was talking all the while, nervous jumble of words, "What the hell man I was just trying to help."

Out in the parking lot I was afflicted by my own nervous jumble of words. "Oh, help, right, you were trying to help." Now I am squatting beside my car in a dark, rain-steamy parking lot, tapping my forehead against the front quarter panel of the old rusty Nissan we bought together, repeating with the zeal of the clock-radio choir these words: *I cannot do this can't do it don't want to do this without you.*

I don't know for how long: until my nose smashed against the metal and my face went funny-bone numb and I was dropped in a dusty dodgeball field back of my grade school, lying in the infield inhaling the rubber of the ball that hit me and repeating that strange-to-me-then word I remembered seeing printed across the ball. Voit. Voit.

"What'd he say?" The voice was nasally but curious. Another voice answered, lower but seemingly female and black.

"Boat? Damn if I know."

"He can't do it without his boat," said the nasal-voiced

man. "Now what do you think he can't accomplish without his boat?"

"Voit," I said—indignantly—and was answered this time with a rib kick. I hit the pavement then. To feign what? Fear? Death? There was nothing left for me to fake. I knew then that since she left I'd faked everything. Or maybe the opposite was true; maybe I did not know emotion until it up and crawled in bed with me right along the same time she up and crawled in bed with her Rick.

I only know I felt more alive, stretched out on the oil-slick pavement, grimacing against the rib kicks, than I had since she left. When the kicks would slow or cease I would scream "Voit!" and soon every bone was numb. My arms and legs stung with pavement scrapes. I smelled that smell—you know the one—the smell of earliest physical pain. Hot rain laced with rust.

"Ain't he about paid?" asked the black woman. Her low, hacking voice concealed a note of sympathy. I wanted to love her for it, but my ribs cried out for more kicks, as if someone had pulled the plug on a song to which I was dancing.

"Not from the sound of him," said the leader. Obviously he knew need from want. But suddenly a new voice spoke up—"Y'all leave off him." The cashier? Strange as it sounds, until then I had not made the connection. I wasn't at all sure this was not something I wasn't doing to myself, or that the weight of my desire had not provoked some miracle posse to torture me.

I opened my eyes, blinked up at the buggy aureole surrounding the yellow streetlight. The cashier stood above me smoking, but he seemed the least of my problems. The nasal-voiced man was dressed in coat and tie, a terrifying outfit for a man choreographing a beating. The black woman was neither: just a skinny shave-headed boy dressed, like me and the cashier, in shorts and T-shirt.

There was talk among them, profane and incomprehensible. I wasn't listening. Beth kneeling beside me, ripping leeches from my skin. I protested hysterically. Beth swathing me in bandages, bedding down beside me in the grocery store parking lot so slick with squashed lettuce leaves and spilt milk.

And then I passed into very familiar territory: boredom. I was exhausted, as I had often been in those days, by my inability to get over the hurt. I knew what I was going to feel before I felt it and it was stifling, sad, for what is death, finally, but not being able to even bring yourself to anticipate a surprise?

"Can I buy y'all dinner?" I said.

Once I heard a teacher say that a sure way to change things was to honor opposite impulses. See where they take you. At the time—I was an impressionable young student with pen poised and mind open—this advice seemed a simple answer to the most difficult question there is: how to get across the room. I wanted to live my life scathed but not bleeding. This was before Beth came and well before she went, ages before such advice on How to Change would have struck me, before I even heard it, as superficial fluff to sell magazines in a checkout line.

Crouched by my car, I remembered that I had never actually tried this tactic, intentionally at least. I was all the time doing things I didn't want to do, and saying the opposite of what I felt, but that was to me the only possible way to live this life.

In the car the man in the tie introduced himself as Darren. The other one, of the shorn head and confusing voice, went unnamed. The clerk had long ago sighed and disappeared inside the market. We drove along the river road toward the Albemarle Sound. I never named a restaurant, for it did not feel as if we were stepping out for a bite. It felt more like they were driving me to their clubhouse, some cinder-block hut down in the swamp bottom, where they would torture me with country music of the black-hat Vegas variety and perhaps a little later, when the bottles grew light, a stun gun. Out the window I watched Bell Island, where the schoolkids once hijacked the ferry that brought them across the sound to school and rode around the inlet smoking dope until the Coast Guard escorted them back in. Bell Island kept pace with the sunken Olds and I imagined the inside of the clubhouse, the club colors draped over cinder block and flanked with porn centerfolds.

"You going to get along all right without your boat?" Darren said.

"V-O-I-T. Like a dodgeball?"

"What a dodgeball has to do with you breaking bad on my boy Kirk I ain't even going ask."

I started in on a meditation about memory, how we all lived in closets cluttered with primal objects of childhood. Rosebud. Beth, come home. In the middle of a sentence I stopped, for we all had stopped—the driver had coasted still in the middle of the road, Darren was half-turned to watch me.

I said, to turn it back on them, "I think maybe what happened was that y'all hurt some part of my brain that stored, you know, old stuff like dodgeballs."

"We ain't hurt shit," said the driver, stepping indignantly on the gas. "You were already fried when we got there."

I fell back into the seat. What could I say? It seemed time to deliver myself to whatever course of action I had set in motion by pushing the cashier in his pliant chest. I thought of a Halloween carnival in grade school, being blindfolded and having my hand plunged into a vat of Jell-O standing in for crushed eyeballs. I believed I laughed a little to myself, a little leak of laughter like air out of a tire, which cemented whatever opinion my companions had of me, for they talked in low, brooding voices and I could not even muster up the energy to eavesdrop.

We arrived finally at a restaurant I did not recognize. I knew only that we were headed south and could feel from the elements, from the song of tree frogs and the lonesome whine of the tires on rough pavement, that we were headed toward the sound. I spent the last few miles of the trip listening to the road-grimy trucker beg for his baby back. Outside it was deep-country black except for a buzzing streetlight leaning above a pier over the water, casting a thin sheen on the rippling shallows. The establishment—from the low, vinyl-sided looks of it, a modular-unit, short-order grill—was obviously closed for the night. Dry-docked trawlers listed precariously in the parking lot. The scene felt illicit, excitedly so, as if we'd come to score drugs or rob someone. I thought, fleetingly, that I had found something to take the place of my fiercely coddled misery but was quickly sucked under by those insipid strings, which dragged me to the bottom of the black sound.

The driver had a key to the restaurant. Darren ordered him

to bring us beers and fry up some shrimp burgers. He said to me, "What the hell do you eat?"

"Not much from the looks of him," called the driver from a kitchen lit only by the lights of freezers he was rooting around in.

"I'm on a diet," I said. A diet with its own sound track. The heartbreak diet.

"The thing about diets is all these people starving to death and these rich fuckers on a damn diet." This line sputtered out from the darkened kitchen.

"Your point?" Darren said to the shadows.

"Ones that can afford to eat lobster every night going around starving. Bet they ain't sending the money they save over to Africa."

The driver brought us beers. I left mine untouched. Darren said, "His point is a good one, wouldn't you say?"

"I'm not rich."

"You're just skinny and stupid."

It seemed time to protest, to ask why we were here, alone in the south end of the county, where not only corpses but corpses still seat-belted into cars turned up in sullen lagoons. But instead I leaned forward and said, "I'm not real hungry."

"Bring him some coleslaw," said Darren. He squinted my way. "What's your problem?"

I said, "What do you mean?" though I knew exactly what he meant.

"Going off on Kirk for no reason, beating your head upside your car. Calling out for some damn dodgeball."

"I guess I'm lonely," I said. He widened his eyes, as if suddenly I had come into focus for him, and I added, "is all."

"You ever had anyone die on you?" he asked, wincing slightly, as if it took great effort to send his words my way.

"Yes," I lied. Maybe this was the worse lie I'd ever told—out of the dozens Beth knew about, the ones that passed undetected. She wasn't dead; I was dead to her, maybe, but she lived and breathed and was at that moment, getting on toward bedtime on a Wednesday night in late spring, no doubt moving against some Rick met at a conference, and the thought of anyone else touching her in the places I discovered made me claim now all degrees of suffering as my own.

"You're lying," he said. The driver set a huge bowl of soupy coleslaw in front of me, a fresh beer for Darren. He laid out the place settings, lining up the fork and knife with a prissiness that amused me, given our surroundings.

"He's definitely lying," the driver said, his words lingering as he disappeared back into the kitchen.

From the kitchen came the hiss of frozen meat dropped into a fryer. I tried hard to summon my song, those strings that had driven me out of the house and into the arms of fate; I tried to focus on the trucker's lament, but the tree frogs, the sibilance of fried meat, the buzz of the streetlights kept my song away.

"You think it's all up to you, don't you?" said Darren.

I thought he wasn't who he said he was. I thought Beth had sent him, or maybe the pathetic trucker wailing away the hours as he tried to scrub away his sins. My comrade in want, sending his messenger to set me straight. I thought Darren was not real and I asked him just who he was to the cashier. Friend? I said. Second cousin?

He looked through me and repeated: "Up to you, huh?"

I shrugged, mindful of what my shrug suggested: that the weight of the world was not upon me.

Darren shook his head, burped, pushed his chair back, summoned his driver, who had been eating back in the kitchen, as if he knew his place in the world.

"Get the bag out of the trunk," said Darren. To me he said, "Let's get."

I rose and followed, queasy from the coleslaw. I was thirsty, too, and exhausted, yet I felt oddly settled. Docility was the answer? I could have apprenticed myself to the migrants, their crooked crew boss, had I only known.

I followed Darren along the pier to its rickety end. I looked to the water's edge, the black sucking sand, beach studded with cypress knees and beyond—a stretch of water poised deceptively as earth. I thought that whatever happened to me then had nothing to do with the slow boy filling in for Deb at the market and everything to do with the times that my vanity had come uncaged in some tavern, dancing with some strange, maneuvering her around the dance floor by her hip bones while Beth scrubbed kitchen tiles and tried not to think of that person she did not want to acknowledge I was capable of up and becoming.

"Take your clothes off," said Darren. I did so without question because I was gone—off on that flight that took me frequently and far back in time: Yeah, but I always came home alone, I was saying to Beth, I never slept with any of them, just a little lip, some here-and-there tongue. Never once betrayed us like you did with him. She did not get to argue the meaning of the word *betrayal*. I did all the talking, and it took all the energy I would have expended on worrying about what I was being asked to do: take off my clothes for a man dressed like he was about to sell me some insurance.

Darren's driver arrived toting a gym bag from which he pulled a tangle of rope, some handcuffs, and greasy lengths of chain. He uncoiled the rope, surveyed my nakedness with scorn.

"I don't relish getting wet over his bony ass," he said to Darren.

"It doesn't appear to be up to you," I said.

This made Darren smile. But the driver, once he had me in the water and pushed hard against the piling at the end of the pier, wrenched the cuffs tight and lashed the ropes.

Above us Darren had fired up a cigar to ward off mosquitoes, but the smoke didn't appear to be working; I heard him swear and slap himself. The driver bound me tighter to the splintery black piling, which smelled of creosote and rotting shellfish. Sound water lapped black and empty just above my shoulders.

"Wait for me in the car," Darren told the driver, and when he was gone, he said, "You know, you brung this on yourself, chief. We wouldn't be here if you hadn't asked us to have supper with you."

"No, actually it was the lottery ticket," I said.

"Either way, you taking some crazy chances."

I thought that this was a good thing, and almost said so, but I realized just before I spoke that I still did not know who Darren was or what he planned to do with me. My situation seemed far worse, on the one hand, than it had just hours before, when I had left for the store. Yet there was this other hand. I could not say what it was. Nor was I even sure

I wanted to know. Would it cure me, and would being cured mean that I would learn to live my life without loving her, wanting her?

There was a silence, then a puff of smoke arrived from above, seething through the space between the slats, clouding about my head.

"So she fucked you over, whoever she is. And now you get to go around feeling righteous, starving yourself, and beating up on grocery store clerks?"

I had an answer to this, but he didn't leave enough space.

"You know something about love, chief?" he said through the smoke. "It makes you scared of every damn thing, you all the time worrying about whether she's going to come back from the store or was I good enough and does her daddy like me and on and on. And at the same time it makes you feel free. That's what it does when it's really cooking, right?"

I waited for a puff of cigar smoke, but there was nothing, only mosquitoes feasting on my cheekbones, my bound hands straining against the rope.

"You saying you didn't feel nothing like that?"

"I did." I do, I thought to say, but I didn't want to give Darren any more ammunition than he could divine by looking at me. He was picking up a lot just looking, and it unnerved me, the way he recognized himself in me, the way he described to the letter the way it felt to love Beth. I did feel scared the whole time I was with her, and yet I felt as free as I'd ever felt. But maybe I was loving her all wrong. Maybe what Darren had described was not love but some kind of copycat ailment with the same symptoms.

"Hell, man, why would you want to feel that way?" Darren said. "Far better to be cooped up in your own head than having to go around scared all the time."

"Who the hell are you anyway?"

"Me? I'm that boy you broke bad on's uncle. I came down expecting excitement, I guess. Find you banging your head on a car and I *know* this motherfucker needs to be put out of his misery."

"That's what this is?"

"This is whatever you want it to be."

"I don't think my desire is being considered here," I said. In answer there came a snort, then footsteps tapping away up the pier. I might have called out, but not to Darren or his driver. Beth. Voit. My trucker, oddly quiet now, as if he'd found some end to his suffering, seen through the loneliness and longing to some sweet levitation.

In time I realized the water was creeping up my neck. I thought of what I knew of tides: they were controlled by the moon, and the moon this night was a pasty scythe blade floating above a line of loblollies and seemed too sickly to perform such a feat.

Sometime in the night I began the story of How We Met, and it began at the beginning, and wound its way around facts as stock and familiar as the items I purchased weekly from the market, until the moon moved lower toward the water and a hazy light appeared in the sky.

Watching the sky, water lapping at my chin, I remembered hearing how they'd discovered that the earth was round: a boat had sailed out to the horizon, kept on moving, out of sight, over the earth's curve. Inching my way up the barnacled piling, I saw how they could get behind such an idea.

Results for Novice Males

Last night, Larry got himself arrested again. The conditions were especially favorable: It was humid out, unbearably so, though a line of thunderstorms had pushed through on their way to the coast, stalling above us for an hour's pummeling. After the storms, people streamed outside—into backyards, onto porches—and Larry had an audience. Down the hill, through the dip of thick wood and unofficial trash dump the neighborhood kids called the Ravine, the projects east of us hummed with thumping bass notes, tire screeches, crazy laughter. Hazy moonlight, bats swirling drunken loops around power lines, skin slaps against mosquito bites. Larry was not wearing a shirt.

I was in the bathtub soaking away the crust of salt, road grime, and sweat from an eighty-mile bike ride when sirens arose from the Ravine, whining closer until blue light streaked across the dark walls above the tub. Had things not soured between us, Larry would have ridden at least a part of those eighty miles with me, for Larry and I used to train together. Three weeks ago, we entered the same race, an Olympic distance triathlon in the foothills, but Larry took offense when I beat him roundly in all three disciplines. Apparently Larry thought racing together meant racing alongside. His swim wave took off three minutes before mine, but Larry is a sluggish and graceless swimmer, and I was out of the water twenty-eight seconds before he hit land. I say "apparently"—it wasn't as if I was aware of passing him, nor could I tell who was who out there. It was a wet-suit-legal race, my goggles were fogged, the lake was tannic-laced, the color of Coca-Cola—all I saw were slick black torsos, fluttering feet, arms arcing in and out of the water.

Larry took it personally. I suppose he thought I'd wait for him. I was out of my wet suit and into my bike shoes and helmet in an absurdly slow four minutes—I even took the time to eat half a PowerBar. Though this was not my first race, I was so anxious about finishing that I erred on the side of endurance rather than speed. I even entered the race in the Novice Male category. Not Larry. It was his first triathlon—he'd never cycled more than twenty-five miles in his life, and he barely trained for the run or swim either—but he insisted on signing up in his age-group classification.

"Novice Male?" he said over the fence one afternoon. "Forget *that*."

I shrugged. "Hell, I'm still a novice. This is only my second season, and I want to save it all for the Ironman."

I'd decided to do a full Ironman race next season. I'd mentioned this to Larry a half-dozen times, but he always smiled and nodded, as if he knew something I didn't, which had to do with my bailing or ending up the season injured.

"Who wants to be called into the water with the novices?" he said. "Everybody turning around, checking you out."

"Actually, we're the last wave, Larry. There will be nobody left to check us out."

"They make you guys go last?" I grinned at the "you guys." "So the winner's like, what, an hour ahead of you?"

I shrugged again. It occurs to me now that when talking to Larry, I communicated mostly with my shoulders.

"It's best if the water's clear. You're less likely to get kicked in the face. You wouldn't believe how turbulent it can be in one of those mass starts."

I'd never experienced a mass start, nor had I been kicked in the face—I always start my swim far to the right and a little behind the rest—but Larry wasn't listening.

"Psychologically, though . . . ," he said.

I waited for him to finish his sentence, but apparently he thought he'd gotten his idea across.

"You know your age group's probably the toughest," I told him. "Most guys don't get into this sport until their late twenties. Takes them a while to mature, especially on the bike. Few years, they're at the top of their game, man. I'll bet the top three go close to two hours."

Larry said, "Guess that's one advantage to getting older."

I grinned again. Shrugs and grins: the language I share with old across-the-fence Larry. "Oh, my age group isn't exactly slow."

"So what's your goal?" he asked me.

Like most Novice Males, I had two goals. The first—the one I made public—was just to finish without embarrassing myself. The second—the one I kept to myself, especially around people like Larry—was to go under two hours and forty-five minutes.

"I've told you, Larry. I'm out there to have a good time and cross the finish line and still be able to walk to the medical tent."

"You're full of shit, Patrick. You know you got a goal. I don't get this modesty thing, man. Might as well just put it out there."

I grinned at Larry, stifling a shrug.

LARRY WASN'T THE KIND of person I'd usually choose to spend time with. He sold couches in the showroom of a discount furniture store, and I practiced law in Raleigh, an hour commute on the interstate. Had I met Larry a few years ago I would have barely tolerated him; a conversation like the one we had about race categories would have led to my avoiding him forever.

But I was a different man a few years ago. I had no understanding of humility, of selflessness—despite my occupation, which contrary to popular belief calls for inordinate amounts of patience, I was not a patient man—and I could not force myself to suffer fools at all, much less gladly. Larry is a fool, but I'm a snob and can be as self-absorbed as Napoleon. I have two children by two women, and I left the second woman for someone quite a bit younger than her, which set the two children and their mothers against me with a vengeance. The younger woman and I had moved here to this quaint, pre-Revolutionary mill town, bought a modest mill house and set about restoring it. We were here for a year when the younger woman, whose name I do not utter aloud anymore, left me for a fellow much closer to her own age.

I'd never been left before; always I'd done the leaving. Instantaneously I went from being someone who does not suffer fools gladly to the worst kind of self-pitying, drunken fool. For a year I sleepwalked through everything, and everything suffered. My job, my relations with my children—a son just out of college, living the ski-bum life in Telluride and a daughter just now entering high school in Raleigh. I failed to return my son's Sunday night calls, and on the weekends I was to host my daughter I excused myself with lies, holed up in my half-refurbished house, drank Maker's Mark by the gallon and listened to Vic Chesnutt CDs my dear departed ex had given me in an attempt to update my classic rock musical tastes.

Listening to Vic Chesnutt while bolting back Maker's Mark is nearly as lethal as mixing barbiturates with the same elixir. Nevertheless I kept it up for eleven months, until my ex-wives alerted my two older brothers—also members of the legal profession—who appeared at my door one Saturday in a rental car, packed a suitcase for me, and drove me to a clinic in the mountains just south of Asheville, where I shook and sweated and seethed with resentment for the requisite twenty-eight days, after which just enough clarity descended for me to ponder my brothers' decision to rent a car to transport me to purgatory. Obviously I was a vomit risk. They might as well have been wearing surgical gloves, so apparent was their disgust for the mess I'd made of my life, but they dealt with the situation efficiently, in clearly billable hours.

Shame is what kept me drinking for that disastrous year after I got left; shame, after I emerged from the clinic, was quadrupled. My brothers fixed things with the firm—that was easy enough—but I had promised to attend ninety meetings of a certain self-help group in ninety days, and I did hang in there, rather gallantly I think, for eight consecutive nights in various dank church basements around our mill town. I confess, however, that I spent more time studying the decor of Protestant "fellowship halls"—the obligatory pictures of Jesus looking like a Blind Faith–era Eric Clapton, the bulletin boards lined with construction paper featuring photos of parishioners descending on long folding tables of casseroles and pound cakes—than I did listening to the monologues of the fellow addicted. The program and I failed to click. It wasn't my snobbishness that prevented the connection, for I make no distinction between a truck driver making public his every vanity and fear and a philosophy professor, though in general, for the sake of entertainment and the time-honored appeal of the vernacular over the genteel, I will go with the truck driver. I admire, from an intellectual distance, the impetus behind those dozen steps, for who can convincingly argue against the need for all of us to operate less out of that black center of self?

I just needed to find another way of going about it, which I did in time. Triathlon, I read once in a cycling magazine, is the perfect sport for aging white men with too much time and money on their hands. My reasons for loving it have to

do with the obsessiveness it requires. It is a most unforgiv-
ing mistress, as they say of the law, though I never found the
law to be anything more than, to extend the metaphor, an
occasional lay. Training for a triathlon requires three concentrated meticulously planned workouts in each of the three
disciplines per week. It fills countless hours, it distracts you
from nearly everything in its path—in short, it is the perfect
remedy for a lovelorn problem drinker trying to learn how to
absorb full on the brunt of life's pain.

Triathlon is all about suffering, of course, though its
particular stripe of suffering leads to a endorphin-enriched
plateau that feels, compared with other avenues of suffering
I have embraced, relentlessly spiritual. If it is true that the
depravity of modern man stems from a spiritual deficiency,
triathlon, if approached from the right angle, will wing your
sculpted, shorn body to nirvana.

Larry Edwards did not approach triathlon from the right
angle. He did not approach many things from the right angle,
I thought last night when the blue lights cast their circular
sweep across my walls. It is my custom, after a long bike ride,
to put on some music, turn out all the lights, and soak for an
hour or so in the whirlpool tub my up-to-date ex-girlfriend
insisted on having installed in the bath we added to the back
of the house. She also insisted on an outdoor shower, which

after she left I avoided not because I was initially against the extravagance and the impractibility (we *do* have a winter in North Carolina) but rather owing to the early evening showers we took there, after our runs, sunlight and fresh heavy air arousing us, Larry Edwards no doubt spying on us from his side of the fence. When she left me, Larry said, "Man, I were you I'da held on to that one." As if she were a car I'd sold. As usual we were perched on the fence, and after I told him she'd moved out (which he knew already, since he'd sat on his porch and watched the U-Haul come when I was deliberately out of town), he nodded toward the redwood slats of the outdoor shower and added, "So, what are you going to do with that thing now, store your mower in it?"

For a good ten minutes last night I enjoyed the play of blue light across the walls, thinking of Larry, of how I'd ended up entangled with the guy. I reminded myself that we had nothing in common except that he happened to own a house next to mine. An accident of timing and geography, like nearly everything else in my life. I was legally drunk when I met the woman who would later leave me, and though she came to hate my drinking, she once told me that she was glad I had overindulged the night we met, for if not I might never have had the courage to approach her (she knew exactly where my courage came from) and we would never have had our year and a half of passion. After she'd been gone a few months, I realized that this chain of events stretched further than she admitted, for if I had not had a few drinks and approached her, had she never moved to the mill town with me, she would also never have changed jobs and started working at the nonprofit where she would meet the younger (though decidedly less fit) man she took off with. We tend to interpret chance in our lives in the most positive light until something happens to remind us that there is always a more threatening version of events shadowing whatever fortune we claim.

The threatening version of events unfolding next door had precedence. Larry has a problem with what they now call anger management. He gets a little sloshed on weekends and takes things out on his wife and children.

I heard the screams last night, in fact, but I ignored them until Larry's shouts grew louder and were joined by other male voices—policemen, obviously—overusing the word *sir*. Then a woman's screechy cries. I knew that the entire block—half of which was gentrified, the other half natives, descendants of or current mill workers—would be outside taking in the show. I like to believe that I'm above such behavior, but there was something about Larry's misfortune that I reveled in. I got out of the tub, toweled off, wrapped the towel around my waist, stained the floorboards with wet footprints on my way to the dining-room window.

They were in the yard—three policemen, Larry, his wife, Barbara—and Larry, from what I could tell, was not cooperating. I couldn't see very well, and so I slipped outside on the porch, forgetting that I was wearing only a towel, that I was still dripping from the bath. The cops were attempting to calm Larry so they could put him in cuffs. Despite the "sirs" I could tell from their accents that they were hometown boys, acquaintances of Larry and Barbara—Larry's high school sweetheart—and that they were not terribly excited about hauling Larry off to jail.

But it was their job to do so, and after a few more tense minutes they cuffed Larry, and talked softly to him, as if he were a child, before leading him to the car. It was then that he saw me. I suppose there was more light out than I thought, for Larry sneered at me in exactly the same way he had when I'd suggested he register as a Novice Male. Then he said something which traveled across the yard in an uncharacteristically husky, phlegm-flecked half cough: "Couldn't even wait to get dressed?"

The policemen and Barbara turned to stare. I knew that Larry would not remember this moment, and that Barbara, as soon as the blue lights switched off and the cruisers moved down the street, would call me on the phone and ask me to go down to the magistrate's office and get her husband out of jail. She'd done so before; even though I tried to tell her I don't practice criminal law, she had it in her head (no doubt from television, which is where 90 percent of Americans pick up their erroneous ideas about my profession) that you call a lawyer to get your husband out of jail when he drinks too much and belts you or one of the kids in the mouth.

I went inside then. As I got dressed, I thought again of how ill suited Larry Edwards is to the sport of triathlon. What he does not realize is that this sport is not really about other competitors. Sure, there are times in a race when I will push myself to pick off the person in front of me, but I'm really competing with myself. This is why I love this sport so, why it's given me what amounts to a new life.

I picked up the phone on the third ring and said, "I'm just getting dressed."

"Thank you, Patrick," said Barbara.

"I need to know what happened, though," I told her.

There was silence so long I envisioned my words crawling the thirty feet from my kitchen to hers.

"He really looks up to you, Patrick." Barbara was crying, and while her sobs got to me, I bristled at her words. Larry, I have always suspected, hates me a little. More than a little, maybe. He hates that I'm a lawyer and he is selling couches for little more than minimum wage. He hates that his high school sweetheart has gained thirty-five pounds while I get to make love to a woman younger than him in the open air of an outdoor shower. He hates that I can afford a set of disc wheels to race in, and Dura-Ace components, a titanium frame Litespeed; he hates even more that I am naturally a stronger swimmer, a smoother pedaler, a faster runner than he is.

"I'm training for an Ironman," I said to Barbara. I have no idea why. Even if Larry had not complained about her attitude toward what little training hours he managed, I would have surmised that she resented it. It left her alone with the kids. It took away precious time he could have spent on a part-time job. Left him too exhausted to help around the house. The yard, the house, their two used ragtag automobiles—everything suffered. On some level I suspected she blamed it on me, who after all had come along and given Larry the idea that this was something he could do.

"Will you get him out?" she whispered. "And then, I'll tell you what"—these words were louder, her tone had hardened, gone crusty, and there was something in her voice that suggested both Larry and I were childish, boorish fools, but that I was the more hopeless case—"tell you what, Patrick, Larry won't bother you again. Okay? I'll see to it."

"Larry's not bothering me," I said.

"Thank you," she said, and hung up. I looked at the phone in my hand and then at my body, as if I had forgotten to get dressed and were still parading around in a towel.

Down at the county jail, after I settled things with the magistrate, Larry appeared, not smiling.

"Where's your towel?" he said. I did not shrug and I did not grin, which suggested to me that my patience was strapped, that I needed to dig deep—as I often have to do on a long training ride, a hot and humid race—to simply keep going.

"I don't want to go home now," said Larry when we were in the car. I stopped myself from telling Larry that he did not get to decide. I did not remind him that I had just bailed him out of jail for assault charges, that I put up my own money to secure the bond only because I was so embarrassed at having been caught gawking at his misfortune wearing nothing but a towel.

What was the right thing to do? Stay out all night driving Larry around town while he drank himself into a state of self-loathing? Was I indulging him, or encouraging his self-indulgence, by not taking him straight home to immediately make his amends? Driving through the still downtown streets, blinking yellow streetlights recalling the earlier swirling blue, I thought about how ill equipped I was to handle this situation. The only thing I knew how to do was run, swim laps, ride my bike. In my training guides and the triathlon magazines I devour they talk about "junk miles"—the mileage one accumulates without actually getting better, stronger, faster—mileage that does nothing to correct mistakes in your form. Most of my life had been spent piling up the junk miles, but what I needed tonight was simply the patience to persevere. Any more—actual wisdom—was too much to ask for from someone who had ridden a hilly eighty miles at a little over eighteen miles an hour.

I told Larry, Look, fine, we don't have to go home right yet, but I'm not going to cart you around if you are planning on doing more drinking. He said the stores were all closed now anyway, and besides he had a better idea. He said he wanted to do a brick.

A brick is a training session where you stack one discipline atop another with only a short, race-simulation transition: bike–run usually but sometimes a swim–bike.

"Tomorrow?"

Larry said, "No, tonight. Right damn now."

I laughed—an actual laugh, sincere, for what he said was funny despite his drunkenness. I told him, You're kidding right? I said, You've been drinking, you're dehydrated, it's the middle of the night, I just got off my bike, I rode eighty miles.

I said there were a dozen other reasons why this was a bad idea.

"Come on, Ironman," said Larry. "You can do it."

I know what I can and cannot do. And for the most part—a staggering 98 percent of the time—I stop myself from doing what I know I can't—should not—do. Those things I know will lead to pain—mine and other people's—I don't do anymore. I no longer take pleasure in making myself feel bad, no longer seek out pain to feel alive. But as they say in those basements, it's progress, not perfection. Every time I heard that phrase I would look over at old Clapton, expecting him to demand perfection. But he never contradicted whoever was rationalizing their failure with a version of those words I trafficked in nigh hourly for years: *I tried.* Seemed to me failure was sanctioned in cases where maximum effort was expended to try and do right. And then, as they said, you simply did the next right thing.

It was not difficult to spin Larry's challenge into what would be the next right thing for him to do. He needed to sweat out the booze, work out his rage. He needed to redeem himself in Barbara's eyes. She would be thankful I'd steered him clear of more Miller High Life.

I said, "How are you going to get your gear out of the house without waking everyone?"

I was not looking at Larry by then because I did not want
to see him—his competitive leer, or worse, the supercilious
smirk suggesting he knew something about me that I did not
know, or want to know, myself.

"I keep everything in the shed," he said.

As soon as I agreed to the brick, implicitly I suppose, by
asking about his gear, guilt set in. I staved it off with logistics:
Where would we swim? We'd have to wait until daylight to
ride. It made no sense and I said so, but Larry had answers.
We'd jump the fence at the city pool—he and his buddies had
been doing it since they were in junior high, they'd never been
caught—and there was enough moon out to keep us safe on
the traffic-less country roads surrounding our town.

"Where are we riding?" I asked.

"Shull's Mill."

Shull's Mill was the hilliest, curviest training ride within
fifty miles. I always avoided it unless I was feeling particularly masochistic. Larry claimed he did hill repeats out there,
though you couldn't tell it by his legs.

"I don't think this is such a good idea," I said as I pulled
into the alley behind our houses.

"What's the problem?"

"You seem like you got something to prove." I turned the
engine off, but neither of us made a move to get out.

"And you don't?"

I allowed myself to look at him then, because he'd pissed me off.

"No, Larry. I don't have a damn thing to prove by pulling a brick in the middle of the night with my drunk neighbor I just bailed out of jail. Don't have anything to gain by it either."

"Never known you to turn down a chance to train."

"You've never gotten hammered, slapped one of your kids around, gotten yourself in and out of jail, and come over to the house in the middle of the night asking me to do a brick with you after I rode eighty miles, either."

I knew I'd gone too far judging by the silence, which was of the stunned variety, like the quiet a small child suffers after a particularly hard fall.

Larry said finally, in a creaky register that suggested near tears, "I thought it would be good for me. Like, you know, get all this out of my system. You know I really look up to you, Patrick. I seen how you worked yourself out of the same damn hole I'm in just by training."

The same damn hole as Larry? I thought of the outdoor shower, of how today was the day to finally reclaim it. How wonderful it would feel to come home at daybreak after a hard workout and stand there in the rising sun, serenaded by bird chirp and the baritone thrum of trucks out on the highway. It seemed I had the chance to get beyond things, that one fairly easy workout lay between me and some place that I'd been swimming, cycling, and running toward since she left.

"A training brick, right? Not a race."

Larry said, "What kind of race would it be, shape I'm in? Talk about your level playing field."

There was no such thing—we both knew that—which was partly why we disliked each other so much.

In the kitchen, filling water bottles, I glanced at the bulletin board where I had pinned race schedules, my training logs, and my times for last season's races, which arrived in the mail on a sheet entitled "Results for Novice Males." Once Larry, having followed me inside, spent an uncomfortably long time studying my training logs (I recorded everything there—times, distances, interval reps, average speed, intensity, average heart rate), and said, pointing to the heading on my official race results, "Why don't you at least snip off that part?"

Because wielding a pair of scissors will not transform me into an Elite Male, I wanted to say. Instead I believe I shrugged.

We'd agreed to meet in the alley behind our houses. I loaded my gear into the back of my Cherokee and waited for Larry. Lights went on in what I knew to be his kitchen. I braced myself for shouts. In a few minutes, Larry came out dressed in a Speedo and a bike jersey, a backpack slung over his shoulder. He met me five minutes later, pushing his bike out of the shed.

"I thought you said your gear was in the shed."

"You were spying on me?"

"Was Barbara up?"

"Didn't want her to worry. I told her about your plan."

"My plan?"

"Relax. She thinks you hung the damn moon. Lawyer and all. If I tell her you think a workout's what I need she'll swear on the Bible it's the only way. If I was to tell her it was my idea, she'd be calling the law before I could get my tires pumped up."

I don't know why I was always second-guessing my neighbor's motives, when for years I excused my own mistakes with a phrase: *I wasn't thinking*. Most of the time the phrase should have read, *I wasn't thinking of anyone but myself*. Everything Larry did, however—especially last night—seemed designed to put me in an awkward position. Telling Barbara this brick was my idea seemed insurance should something awful happen.

Driving to the pool, Larry's beery breath filled the car, reminding me of the high likelihood that something awful could happen. There is no worse odor than booze fumes seeping from the pores of someone sweating out a drunk. I breathed through my mouth to escape it, rolled down the windows to let in the heavy, humid air.

We did not talk, did not even whine, as triathletes often do before a hard workout, about lack of training, injuries, bad diet decisions—those reasons we cultivate to excuse poor performance. Silently we set up our transition area by the car, just outside the cyclone fence we'd have to jump. We were going over the cycling route when Larry mentioned the run.

"Run? Isn't that a little ambitious?"

"Not for you, Ironman."

"Swim–bike seems plenty given the circumstances."

"Let's say I got a lot to prove."

I didn't care for the sound of this. But I stripped to my bike shorts, grabbed my goggles, and struggled over the fence, knowing that I'd feel better once the swim started.

The water felt preternaturally warm, amniotic almost. Debris from the storm—leaves, sticks, trash—floated on the surface. Nevertheless I did feel better once submerged. Of the three disciplines, swimming is probably my favorite, for I feel the least amount of self-consciousness in the water. This isn't to say that I'm particularly fast. I'm usually in the top third of the Novice Males, which means that in a race I'm swimming by myself or alongside a couple of others. But Larry drafted behind me for the entire one thousand yards. I felt strong in the water, fluid and relaxed, and after five hundred yards I accelerated to lose him, but he kept in my wake, his hands brushing my feet every few strokes. He'd veer off at the wall, but as soon as I emerged from my flip there he'd be, hard behind me. I could not shake him.

He was into his bike shoes and helmet before I was. Surely his quickest transition ever; I was sipping water, wiping my feet with a hand towel, and Larry was running for his bike. We did not speak at all—well, I did, said something about his swim, complimented him on keeping up with me, but he only huffed, obviously winded, and applied himself to transition.

I let him go. I'd catch up with him when Shull's Mill lifted itself in lazy lariat curls from the flats along the river, rising and tightening its hairpins until the grade was upward of 18 percent, when I'd resort to the granniest of bottom-ring granny gears, the lactic acid beginning its icy burn through my calves and quads.

And this is exactly where I caught him, on the first hard climb. He was standing up on his pedals, weaving wildly; I stayed seated, dropped my heels, slid back in the saddle, concentrated on spinning a decent cadence, blew past him on the penultimate switchback. That seemed the end of the evening. He would not even attempt the run; I looked back at him, took note of his wobbling, his upper body thrown over the headset, his pedal stroke deteriorating into desperate chops. He'd spent everything in the water. Keeping up with me was killing him.

This is not a race, I reminded myself as I settled into the climb, struggling quite a bit actually, and why the hell not? I'd ridden eighty miles, had no sleep, it was just light enough out to see five feet in front of me, no way of avoiding potholes, gravel, debris from the storm. It hit me how dangerous this was around the time that Larry, out of the saddle again, his thick legs pistoning, his breathing echoing through the hollow, whooshed past me on the final hairpin.

Again I let him go. Obviously he needed this more than I did. I am at a place in my life where I don't need to win, as my unapologetically Novice status attests. Didn't I let my brothers cart me off in a rental car to the clinic without protest? Didn't I let she-who-shall-remain-nameless take off with her younger man? Larry would have behaved badly in both situations, would have denied, protested, fought, ended up in jail.

As he shot out of sight I remembered the time I let him talk me into joining a group ride organized by the local bike shop. He argued that it would be good for us, make us faster, improve our bike-handling skills, and because I'm a nice guy I caved. But triathlon cycling is time-trialing—you aren't allowed to draft, you must pass in fifteen seconds or risk penalty—and the few times I rode with the group, I longed to be riding alone, slung out over my aerobars, tucked in against the wind instead of anxiously monitoring the rear wheel of the cyclist six inches in front of me. Despite what Larry thinks, we are not in this together.

The descent on Shull's Mill is tricky in broad day, but at night, after a storm has shaken loose the overhanging canopy, well, we had no business there. I knew that well before I saw Larry hit some blown-down object in the curve ahead, I knew it before I ever trained with the man, the first time he engaged me in his over-the-fence bravado.

He went down on his right side, the bike dragging sideways beneath him. Larry and bike came to rest on the lip of the ditch. When I got to him his teeth were chattering, though it was muggy out and we had both soaked our jerseys with sweat on the climb.

I checked his helmet, which did not appear to be cracked, took note of the road rash raw and beading with droplets of blood on his arm and leg.

Helping him out of his shoes, I asked him what hurt.

"Fuck you," he said.

I reached for his left shoulder and he drew back his arm; the other one, the right, the one he fell on, hung loose and useless at his side.

"Go on," he said. "Get back on your bike."

"It's your collarbone?"

"Don't worry about me. Worry about the clock."

"I'll go get help," I said. Grimacing, he asked for his water bottle. I gave him mine. He'd brought only one, as usual. He was never prepared.

I left him there, hammered the mostly downhill five miles back to town. There was a convenience store near the city limits that stayed open all night long, and I'd planned on stopping there, but when I rounded the bend and saw the store, lit by yellow fluorescence and neon beer and cigarette signs, I kept on going. The most appealing thing about triathlon is the fact that you have three separate disciplines, each with its own set of skills. If you do poorly in the water, you can prove yourself on the bike; if you blow the bike, and can get into your stride within the first mile, you can make up lost time on the run. In this way it is not at all like real life, which seems to me filled with single chances, repetitive mistakes, junk mileage.

I suppose this was what I was thinking when I wheeled into the parking lot of the community pool, hopped off my bike, stripped off my helmet and bike shoes, struggled into my Asics and took off running.

Later I would claim, simply, I wasn't thinking. But this was not true at all. As I ran, I was conscious of the life I had ahead of me, of how, considering the mess I'd made of things up to that moment, it was far better for me to err on the side of endurance. I was thinking about how insincere and hurtful it is for me to pretend to be there for people I don't much care for. I was raised to be nice to people, but nice isn't always what people need.

Leaving Larry by the side of the road felt awkward and unnatural, like trying to run right off the bike always feels. But in time my stride lengthened, my breathing eased, and I felt good enough to settle into my race and concentrate on the next mile, and the one beyond that, until I knew I could not only finish, but finish strong.

Michael Parker's most recent novel, *If You Want Me to Stay,* was a Book Sense Pick for 2005 and winner of the Goodheart Prize for fiction. His previous books include *Hello Down There,* a *New York Times* Notable Book and a finalist for the PEN/Hemingway award, and *The Geographical Cure,* a collection of stories, winner of the Sir Walter Raleigh Award. His work has appeared in the *New York Times Magazine,* the *Washington Post,* and the *Oxford American,* and his fiction has been anthologized in *The O. Henry Prize Stories,* the *Pushcart Prize Stories,* and *New Stories from the South.* He is a professor in the MFA writing program at the University of North Carolina at Greensboro.

A Conversation with Michael Parker

This is your first story collection in more than a decade. Why did these take the form of stories instead of a novel?

I'd written some of these stories, over the past ten years, before I had the idea to collect them. It just turned out that they shared thematic ideas. Or maybe it didn't just "turn out." Some writers argue that you don't choose your subject matter — it chooses you. I wrote several novels in the last decade, and all of these novels had in common at least some of the subject matter that the stories have. Everything I write seems to touch on the notion of love, what it means, how that meaning shifts, how we negotiate its currents. But I never thought of turning these stories into a novel, because they came to me as story ideas, and I'm hard-pressed for story ideas. When I get one, I sit down and roll with it. I'm scared it's going to get gone if I don't.

Do you see yourself in a particular lineage of writers? Since you're from the South, you're in the shadow of writers like Faulkner and O'Connor. Though you love these writers, do you ever want to tell people to quit asking the question?

Well, if I was so ungrateful as to tell people which questions they can and can't ask, I guess I'd have to tell you not to ask me this question. The only reason I find it difficult is that once you've been asked a question a few hundred times, whatever comes out of your mouth in answer seems overly scripted, artificial. I'm always trying to find a new way to answer the question, which is dumb, because I feel about it now the same way I did when I was first asked it twenty years ago. I do love many Southern writers, but I don't read them exclusively, and when I sit down to work, I'm not thinking of them or my connection to them. I have in mind a character and a situation, and that's all. The landscape of my work is 90 percent Southern because that's the landscape I know well. I don't have to make it up. I have to make it fit the desires and shifting needs of the characters, but I don't have to create it out of thin air. I think reviewers that mention it are mostly not from the South. The reviews I get from Southern publications just talk about the people — usually how messed up they are. People want categories. They want to say that this book is like that book, this band is like that band. That's why I'm so fond of the movie *Spring Break Shark Attack*. It's absolutely beyond comparison, and not in a good way, though you have to admit the title is brilliant.

In "What Happens Next," Charlie has made a habit of confessing a story about himself to women, but in truth he tells the story to gauge women's worthiness. That confession becomes a way of controlling what will happen next. But of course the real power lies with the woman — in her evaluation of Charlie's story. What are you saying about the nature of power in a relationship even in its most intimate moments? Is there really no point at which the power struggle between men and women ceases?

Charlie Yancey, I suspect, is like the rest of us in the way that he can make a confession — which is often thought of as an act of contrition, or at least a responsibly adult means of owning up to your mistakes — into something else altogether. But he retains his vulnerability, I believe, because Charlie — again like the rest of us — is pretty apprehensive about what will happen next, especially in relationships. He's failed repeatedly at love, and he thinks if he "controls" the narrative, he doesn't stand to lose as much. But as you point out, the listener has the real power, as she — and the reader, ultimately — understands that Charlie's storytelling has a purpose, and the selection and distribution of image and detail, the words he puts in his mouth and others', are carefully considered. She sees what Isaac Babel in one of his stories calls "the secret curves between the straight lines of prose."

Is there no point at which the power struggle ceases? Yikes! I suspect the most honest answer to this question is, no, probably not. That doesn't mean that love always has to be contentious. Relationships are narratives, and it's inevitable that with the merging of two realities, both parties are going to attempt to control the narrative. This tension isn't deadly (though it can be for people like Charlie, who don't know when to stop); in fact, it's the opposite. It's just life.

In "Everything Was Paid For," though Clay claims to be avenging the wrongs done to his girlfriend by reminding Neal of them daily, the relationship between Clay and Neal becomes more crucial than between Clay and Linda. As this story illustrates, relationships between the men in a woman's past can be as intense as the relationship itself. Can the tension between a current lover and an ex-lover ever end?

In a healthy relationship, yes. But even in a healthy relationship there are ghosts. One of the good things about being older is that you just accept that the people you love have been with others before you. You don't envy the dead and gone so much as you might when you're Clay's age, though, true, you hear them rattling around in the attic.

Clay's relationship with Neal is based on exploitation and revenge. He actually convinces himself that he's avenging his girlfriend's honor by extorting goods from this guy who treated her badly in the past. He has a skewed sense of honor, and a lot of this has to do with desperation. He's just a kid, and he's made some bad decisions, and now he has bills to pay and what seemed like fun — playacting with Linda, masquerading as adults — has become a terrible burden. Only when he's truly, physically trapped — in the heating duct beneath the drugstore — does he realize what he's done, how horribly he's treated her.

But back to the question: I don't think it's only men who carry on an active relationship with their lovers' ex-lovers. Most of the stories in this book are from a male's point of view because I happen to know that side of the river better than the far shore. But I don't think the responses and actions of all the male characters are exclusively male. I don't know that a woman would go to the lengths that Clay does to "protect" her lover's honor, but the impulse to manipulate a situation, especially when you're desperate and confused — I don't think you have to be a man to think that way.

"Hidden Meanings, Treatment of Time, Supreme Irony, and Life Experiences in the Song 'Ain't Gonna Bump No More No Big Fat Woman'" has become one of your most popular stories. Why do you think that is? What is it that people love about this story so much? And what was the process of writing it?

Well, there's the title of the song, for starters, for which I owe the venerable Joe Tex. And perhaps the form itself is familiar to most readers, who have surely had to write a paper for a teacher whose approach to the topic — not to mention attitude toward the students — annoyed them to no end. But I like to think that if that story touches people, it's because of its shifts. It moves from comic to seriocomic to tragic, and returns to a lighter, more seriocomic note. Of course, these tonal shifts weren't in the first draft, which came more quickly than anything I've ever written. I heard that song on the radio, and I thought it might be amusing if someone took that song — obviously a novelty song, of no real import except to entertain — as a serious comment on social discourse. Initially I pitched it in the comic vein, but when I looked it over I thought (as I so often do when looking over a first draft) "so what?" It needed more weight, a moment of gravity and, overall, a deeper level of desire. So I added the stuff about the father, and tinkered quite a bit with the sentence rhythms in that section, and the story came together at last.

"The Right to Remain" is told from the point of view of Sanderson, who is stalking his ex-girlfriend. Yet we never hear a word from her and she is never even given a name, obviously conscious choices on your part.

Surely she has a story, and no doubt it's an interesting and vital one. It would be easier to tell the story of the person who has been victimized, as opposed to the person who is doing the victimizing. I guess I took the same approach in "Everything Was Paid For." These guys are making huge mistakes; they're committing crimes, really, but they're not completely evil people. Sure, they're unlikable, but they act out of some notion which is often referred to as "pride." Sanderson feels like he's been disrespected both by his ex and her new lover, so he is able to justify his actions by avenging his wounded pride. Clay, too, feels like his pride has been compromised, even though what happened to Linda before he met her has nothing at all to do with him. You hear people say, of themselves and of others whose actions they seek to defend, that they "have a lot of pride." It seems to me that this idea of pride gives them license to be clueless as to the effects of their actions on other people. At least in these two cases, pride instigates acts that are selfish and self-destructive. I'm not judging them, though nor am I cutting them any slack. Both characters, to my mind, begin to understand how low they've sunk.

Most of these stories, with the exception of "What Happens Next" and "Everything Was Paid For," begin after a relationship has ended. Why do your stories often begin after the end? What is it about that point that makes this the critical beginning of things? Is there something that the men see, or think they see, that they didn't before?

That's an interesting observation, one I wasn't aware of. I did hear someone say, quoting from a self-help book, that men grieve for dying relationships after they're over, while women go through the stages during the actual death. Do all men suffer from delayed onset of the bleeding heart? I doubt it, though a good number of these guys seem to finally take stock of things after they're well over.

I think I was interested in the idea of a relationship as narrative, and the ways in which the narrative is constantly being rewritten after it's over, which is not, as is commonly thought, a "lie," but rather a part of the process of healing, and of learning to love more responsibly.

Music seems to run through all of your stories, either explicitly or implicitly, so much so that you were able to construct a kind of dream soundtrack for this collection.

To me, one of the most valuable and vulnerable human artifacts of our day and age is the Breakup Tape. I don't know how they got through heartbreak before the age of recording devices. No, I take that back, because I predate recording devices, and I know how we did it — we either played the same 45 endlessly on our record players until our siblings beat on the walls of our ranch houses, or we called up the same unfortunate late night DJ and begged him to play, just one more time, I swear I won't ask again tonight, "She's Not There," by the Zombies.

Every case of heartbreak seems to have its own distinctive and vibrant soundtrack. I borrowed the title of this collection from Otis Redding's song "I've Been Loving You Too Long (to Stop Now)." And yes, actual songs feature prominently in three or four of these stories. What characterizes love, or the end of it, at least for me, is that terrifying discrepancy between what you feel and what you can articulate. I love music because it expresses the inexpressible, and it does it so swiftly, with such force and accuracy.

What do you like least about being a writer?

I wish you would ask me what I love about it, so I could tell you how much time I spend in my pajamas, which is my uniform, though I confess I used to work at a place where my name was stitched in red thread above my breast pocket and I wish I could find some writing pajamas that allowed me to identify myself similarly.

I'm not real crazy about those panels they put you on at literary conferences. I did one a few years ago titled Violence in Contemporary Southern Literature. I believe they put me on that panel because someone died violently in one of my books, or something like that. Anyway, I got to the panel and met the other two panelists, who seemed nice enough. One was a soft-spoken professor type, and the other was this mild-mannered librarian. The panel started with me, and I got up, read an excerpt from my book, sat down and shut up. When it was time for the other guys to read, they both pulled out knives. We aren't talking pocketknives, either. I confess I felt real dumb, because all I had to prove myself with was a dang pencil.